LOVE YA...

XO!

Rachel
Blanton

BREAK POINT

BREAK POINT

rachel blaufeld

Edited by
Pam Berehulke
www.bulletproofediting.com
Proofread by
Virginia Tesi Carey
Cover design by
© Sarah Hansen, Okay Creations, LLC
www.okaycreations.com
Cover Image
Eric Battershell Photography
Cover Model
Burton Hughes
Formatted by

E.M.
TIPPETTS
BOOK DESIGNS
www.emtippetsbookdesigns.com

AUTHOR'S NOTE

This story began as a novella, part of an anthology with all proceeds going to ProLiteracy. It wasn't until I was about two-thirds of the way through writing it that my beta readers demanded more, so I did something I've never done before.

I left my readers hanging, ending my novella in a cliffy.

It was true—Drew and Jules's story couldn't be finished in a novella. They deserved a full book. In fact, Drew and Jules were so amazing, they needed two happily-ever-afters.

So that's what I gave them.

If you read the anthology, I apologize for making you wait for the full story. But I had to wait in an effort to raise as many funds as possible for ProLiteracy. Thank you again for helping others.

If you're lucky enough to be reading a release-week copy of this book, one dollar of every sale will be donated to a local women's shelter. So, thanks are necessary one more time!

Important: This book includes two bonus chapters (Prologue and Chapter 10.5) in Part One, so if you read the novella, you don't want to skip Part One here.

Last, but not least, this book goes back to Hafton University, the setting for *Vérité* and *Dolce*. It's not necessary to read those books first.

This book is for all the single mothers out there. You brave on your own what most of us can barely do with a partner.

Thank you for raising our future leaders, athletes, musicians, teachers, innovators, and authors, the next generation that will make our world a better place for everyone.

.

PART ONE

PROLOGUE

Jules

I t was a breezy day in late March. Gray clouds folded over the sky, blocking the sun. The temperature was mild for this time of year in Ohio, and sweat dripped down my back as I beat the living hell out of the wall in front of me.

With the ball, of course.

I'd lost track of how many forehands I'd done. Probably two hundred. My shoulder ached, and my palm was a sweaty mess from gripping the racquet. Tossing the grip into my left hand, I wiped my right hand clean on my shorts before grabbing a loose ball off the ground. Like a robot, I began punishing my other shoulder with one-handed backhands.

"Excuse me, are you going to be using the wall much longer?"

Looking up, I saw a guy. Yuppie, mid-twenties, slim but muscular, brown hair underneath his Ivy League hat, and a worn gray T-shirt.

"I'm actually finished," I replied, leaning over to snag a few stray balls and my racquet cover from the ground.

"I didn't mean to make you leave." His eyes bore down on me—chestnut brown, warm, and inviting.

Kindness radiated from him, which was something I hadn't experienced much of recently. I didn't know if I wanted to run from it or snatch it in my grasp and never let go.

"It's cool. I actually have something I need to do." I decided on the former. Running felt safer.

Plus, I do have something. Something I don't want—at least, I don't think I do. Who knows?

My mind was like that nursery rhyme . . . five little monkeys jumping on the bed, until one fell off and hit his head, or however it went. My ideas pinged and bounced about my brain until eventually they all fell flat like worn-out tennis balls.

"You're pretty good." The stranger cocked his head toward the wall, telling me he saw my earlier battle with the concrete slab.

I shrugged. My response wasn't exactly inviting, but he pushed on.

"I just moved here from Boston. Do you live nearby? We could play one day."

It was the first conversation I'd had with the opposite sex since the incident. I should have been more exhilarated or frightened, but instead I felt nothing. Standing here talking with this guy, I felt absolutely nothing.

"I'm working for the new tech company close to the university, app development. I haven't met too many people," he said, his matching Ivy League long-sleeved T-shirt stretching tightly over his chest. On paper, this guy must have been a catch.

Except my head was as cloudy as the sky. His forthrightness and honesty did nothing for me. Most young women would jump into this white knight's arms, but I'd learned to be cautious.

"Um, I'm not sure," was about all I could come up with in the moment.

"No pressure. I go in late on Tuesdays, so I usually come over here and hit. Maybe you'll be back next week."

"Maybe. I might be going back to school . . . college," I offered without further explanation.

"Either way, the invitation stands."

Mr. Ivy League opened his can of balls, slipped his Prince racquet out of its case, and began stretching. He twisted from side to side at the waist, working out the kinks in his lats, taking his racquet with him.

"See you," I called out when I caught a glimpse of bare skin above his shorts. Sadly, I didn't feel a tinge of desire, or anything really.

Walking back to my childhood home, I made a mental note to never hit at the park on Tuesdays. My high school coach had been begging me to come play, to hit a few balls or whatever. His offer was starting to appeal to me. Especially on Tuesdays.

As I walked back into my house, a voice called from inside, "Hurry up, Juliette. The new coach will be here soon, and this isn't something we can pass up."

"Okay, Mom. I hear you."

"I don't think you do," she said as she walked down the steps, a cup of tea in her hand and a smile fixed on her face. Genevieve Smith cared about two things: my dead father, and getting me educated and out.

She'd isolated me from my peers most of my life with constant tennis lessons and tutors to ensure I did well in school, all in the hope of getting a scholarship. Then I'd squandered my first one. It was time to forget all that monkey business and move on. That's what she'd said when she took away my phone and the small life I'd created before it all went to hell. This time around, she meant business.

"I hear you, Mom. Now I need to shower and hurry back down, so if you wouldn't mind . . ."

With my hair still tied in a messy knot on top of my head, I scrubbed myself clean—showers had become perfunctory—and threw on a burgundy off-the-shoulder sweatshirt and black leggings. I dragged some mascara across my lashes, brushed through my hair, and tossed it back into a messy bun.

I was walking down the stairs when I caught sight of a broad-shouldered figure coming up the walkway. There was a knock at the door as soon as I hit the bottom step.

"Get it, Juliette," my mom called from the kitchen.

Opening the door, I was met with the exact opposite of the guy I'd just met in the park. This one was wearing dark jeans and a polo, and had longish hair, tanned skin, and the bluest of blue eyes.

"Hi. You must be Juliette. I'm Coach King . . . Drew. I took over at Hafton last season. The tennis program," he explained, mistaking my immediate crushing and infatuation for confusion.

The words clogged my throat, embarrassment flushed through my veins, and I was sure my cheeks were the color of my hair. It was the basest of attractions, purely physical, something I'd definitely never experienced.

After all, I was only twenty. That was normal, right?

I wasn't meant to fall like this when I was so young. Who the heck knew? My mom had certainly never prepared me for these things, or helped me navigate them. Her cold, austere parenting style was only warmed by my father when he was alive.

"You were expecting me, right?" The coach cleared his throat and glanced at an oversized watch on his wrist.

Underneath his bad-boys looks was quite a gentleman, no doubt the polished product of a prep school. No match for my sheltered suburban-public-school-educated upbringing.

Kind of like California. As if that wasn't mistake enough—signing up for that West Coast lifestyle—I was falling into some kind of blissful spell over my coach-to-be. We hadn't even spoken more than a few words to each other, and my body was humming as a result of my indecent thoughts.

"Um, hi," I said awkwardly, and added a lame little wave.

My mom picked this moment to come striding out of the kitchen, making an entrance.

"Genevieve Smith." She held out her hand. "And you are?"

"Coach King."

We were all still crowded around the threshold, the chilly air making its way inside, which was fine because I was hotter than a fire in hell. And I should know. I'd been to hell, and I was pretty certain I didn't want to go back.

Until now.

"I thought the coach at Hafton was older?" Looking King up and down, my mom inquired about the older coach as if this was all about her. And like everything in my life, it was.

"You mean Ace, Coach Hall? He retired two years ago. I helped him out for a year, and then they gave me the gig full-time. Actually, I was the one who reached out to you. I saw some kick-ass tape of Juliette playing. Pardon my French."

My mom rolled her eyes at his forthrightness.

I was fascinated with King's white smile, his biceps, and his not-so-muted attitude. Although he could have been muttering, "Blah, blah, blah," for all I knew, and I would have been spellbound. Something naughty and oh-so-right was simmering in him, just beneath the surface, clamoring to get out.

"May I come in?" he finally asked.

"Yes, yes. Come into the kitchen," my mom suggested. She offered cold drinks and left the two of us sitting across from each other at our butcher-block table.

"Tell me about yourself," he said.

I want to swim in your eyes. I haven't had a pulse since I left California . . . until now . . . with you seated in front of me.

I felt all of those soul-infused words deep in my belly and slowly rising in my throat. Before they came bubbling out, I tamped them down.

Instead, I said, "Sophomore status when it comes to sports. Tennis player, twenty, failure."

"Hey."

The deepness of his voice set off a ripple of lust through me. When his hand settled over mine, I stared at his calloused fingers and insanely sexy forearms. I wanted to run my fingertips along the veins and stroke his calluses with my thumb.

"You're going to have a second chance, and I'm going to make it happen."

I nodded, my gaze glued to his hand on mine. When he swiftly pulled back, probably realizing the inappropriateness of his action, I felt barren, empty, dejected. Between the chilly assault in California and my mother's cold attitude, I was drawn to King's warmth and kindness like it was a fireplace on a snowy day.

I tried using Jedi mind tricks to make him put his hand back, but he didn't. He spent the next half hour asking me about how much I'd been playing, and discussing tennis strategy with me. Never once did he bring up the incident at my old school.

"You need to get registered for classes, and I'll text you when I think would be a good time for you to watch a practice."

"I don't text. No cell phone."

"Then I'll call you," he said, standing to leave.

Yes, please.

CHAPTER 1

Jules

"Good job, ladies. Keep it up," Coach King called to the girls I'd been watching hit bright yellow tennis balls against the pale blue sky.

His deep voice carried up the bleachers and rumbled down the meadow behind me. A hot/cold shiver fizzled over me, tickling my spine and other places—from his voice alone.

With every stroke of their racquets, I felt my wrist catch, mimicking the girls' movements, mentally stroking a backhand or a forehand. With every lick of encouragement of his voice, my pulse beat quicker, wishing his words were directed toward me.

And not just on the court.

I hoped this wasn't going to be a problem. Obviously, it was wishful thinking. I certainly didn't need any more problems, but Coach King was proving to be one very big one.

His voice drifted into the air. "Hilary, watch the overswing on your backhand."

Another chill swept over me; I was instantly jealous of another girl's name rolling off his tongue. Coach King, all six feet of him with his messy, wavy blond hair (golden blond, sun-kissed blond, perfect blond), blue eyes like the Mediterranean, and forearms to die for. I knew because when he'd visited me several weeks back, I couldn't stop staring at the veins and muscles running along them. He'd subconsciously flexed, and I had to make sure I wasn't drooling.

Then there'd been the light smattering of golden-blond hairs on his skin. Each time they caught the sunlight streaming through the kitchen window, I couldn't help but stare. He'd been sitting in my kitchen, explaining the merits of the school's tennis program, what they had done since he took over the job as head coach, and what my role would be.

"The school's delighted to be obtaining you," the acceptance letter had said. Like a piece of property.

"Still overswinging, Hilary," he called out, jolting me out of my memories.

Hilary could have been any one of the girls. At the time, I certainly had no clue, nor did I care who she was. She just wasn't me.

The team was quite the homogeneous group—too thin, blond hair scraped back tight in a ponytail, skimpy white shorts painted on long tanned legs.

My thoughts wandered, going to a much darker place, worse than daydreaming about Coach King. Torrents of memories of what similar girls had done at my last school rippled through me, stealing my breath, leaving me in a panic.

I remained still, my arms wrapped around my knees, my jean shorts digging into the space where thigh met crotch as my red hair was whipped around my face by a passing breeze. I breathed in and out, counting backward from a hundred. Taking deep breaths and closing my eyes, I allowed positive energy to burn through me and eat away at the bad.

Giggles wafted from the benches below, near the fountain, and then drifted off as the other girls made their way out of the sports complex. Reality returned. It was present day, not back then when I was helpless.

Today I was in control.

Only after the others left—not that it mattered, I was invisible to them—did the coach nod in my direction and motion for me to come down.

That simple gesture felt like something more. Like I meant more to him than was appropriate for a coach and his student. His head tilted to the side for a beat too long, his gaze rested on me more thoughtfully than it had on the others, and he squinted at me in a way I liked very, very much.

"Think you can keep up with them?" He jerked his head back toward the gymnasium, a smirk twisting his mouth.

I zoned in on his lips and became a sailboat slicing through the sea, jumping into the blue ocean that was his eyes as I made my way down the stairs.

That's your coach, Juliette. Let it be.

"I play singles, so I'm pretty sure I'll hold my own with or without them," I said from the bottom step, allowing my natural confidence to make an appearance. *Hello, ego, my good friend.*

"Yeah, I know. I meant, think you can hold your own with that crowd? In general?"

"I'll be fine. I'm looking forward to it," I lied. I wasn't looking forward to dealing with them. Not today. Not tomorrow.

Though, now that I was in the presence of Coach King—up close and personal, outside, shouting, coaching, wearing shorts—I was more excited than before. His forearms fascinated me all over again. They rippled with strength when he moved, making me wonder what they would look like braced over me.

I pulled my hair back into a messy knot at my nape, allowing the breeze to hit my heated neck. "Thanks for asking me to come and watch."

"I'll let you know when we play in that charity event over the summer, and you can come and meet the team."

"Call the house," I reminded him as I walked away.

Yep, I was still living at home.

Which was a good thing considering how attracted I was to my new so-called mentor.

In July, I formally met the girls—and quickly forgot who was who—at some posh club hosting a doubles tournament for charity. King made them all do it for community-service hours. It looked good for the tennis program, for Hafton University, and for him. Mostly, I thought, for him.

Especially when he changed into a navy-blue blazer and skinny khakis for the cocktail reception. He was every bit the country-club boy—private schooled, well heeled—a former tennis protégé who blew out his knee and was now forced to coach. He probably had a long line of tennis bunnies waiting for him outside his apartment . . . or wherever he lived.

I was grateful he didn't ask me to play in the charity thing.

A, I didn't do doubles. Ever.

B, watching him work the event gave me more time to stare at him as he wandered from court to court, schmoozing and smiling.

I was even more grateful none of the other girls asked for my number.

I needed time to deal with that one.

CHAPTER 2

Jules

I shoved my bike into the rack outside school, slipping the lock around the bars without bothering to lock it up. It was official . . . I was the new chick on campus. Well, only for classes. At the end of the day, I went back home to my mom's place.

Smoothing my jean shorts and straightening my mess of a bun, I walked confidently into the lecture hall. Psychology was first on the menu, followed by Statistics later in the day. Of course, several of my teammates were in Psych; it was one of those cupcake courses taught by a fan of the tennis program. In other words, an easy A that kept the team's average GPA nice and inflated.

"Toast is nice," my old coach used to say. *Nice means nothing in a world of excellence, but fuck it. They want me to get nice As; who am I to argue?*

When no one from the team asked me to sit with them, I looked toward an empty seat in the corner. Did I even expect them to? Why would they?

These girls looked like they could have been together since toddler gymnastics, or their collective first periods and long-gone virginities. While I was the fiery-red-haired newcomer, the transfer from another school. The unknown.

I grabbed my tablet and readied myself to take some notes, or at least look like I was busy paying attention while searching the Internet, when the professor entered the room. Crawford was her name, and she looked about as loose as a nun on Sunday. Tight bun, buttoned-up blouse, pencil skirt to the knees, patent-leather pumps, pantyhose. Well, at least I knew she wasn't sleeping with the coach.

No, he gave off a freakier vibe, and I wasn't going to lie, it was one that had kept me up late into the night. On many nights in my lilac bedroom, wishing I knew where he slept.

Lost in a web of visions of King over me, me under him, us in a sideways position with scissored legs, his hands rough and calloused and mine tied behind me, I didn't hear one word of class until, "Class dismissed."

"Hey, Juliette," one of the blond crew said to me as I left the auditorium.

"Um, hey . . ." I squinted, trying to rack my brain. Which one was she?

"Hilary," she said helpfully.

The infamous Hilary.

There she was in all her glory. Five seven or so, tanned, blue-eyed, corn fed. I'd bet she was from the Midwest. We had a lot of those here at Hafton U in Ohio.

Christ, I'm from the Midwest.

Clearly, I hadn't made much of an effort during the summer to remember anything about these girls, let alone their names.

"How's your first day?" She eyed me curiously, careful not to be too obvious by occasionally looking at her smart phone.

"Uh, good so far. First class. I have a break now. And it's Jules. No one calls me Juliette except for my mother." *And me when I chastise myself.*

"Oh, good. Come with us. We're going over to the gym to grab a quick workout and check out the schedule for the fall tournament."

I didn't want to go, but like a kid drawn to an ice cream truck, I was compelled to see the coach. And I had to work out eventually today.

"All right."

"Come on. Lulu has a car."

Lulu. I'm not shitting you.

I walked out into the late-August heat as Hilary ran off at the mouth

12

about some football party coming up. In a meadow, twinkly lights, some guy named Pierce she was obsessed with . . . it all blurred together. The basketball team ruled the school. Hafton was all about its top-level sports, especially the ones that brought in the big bucks.

"Lu, this is Jules, the new girl. Remember meeting her at the club over the summer?" Hilary said. She opened the front passenger door and slid in while I crawled into the backseat like it was death row.

Lulu, her hair with its expensive highlights slicked back in a low ponytail, turned her gaze on me. Her dark green eyes bore into mine. "Yep, where'd you come from again?"

"I was playing out in California. Didn't work out, so I came closer to home." It was mostly the truth.

The two of them might as well have been twins in their olive-green short-shorts and white tanks, and Tory Burch flip-flops on their feet. My cutoffs felt less-than, like me.

We pulled out of the parking lot, and Lulu spoke to me in the rearview.

"King's got a major hard-on for you. All he talked about was the new singles player he was getting. Stacia was getting kind of pissed. She used to be his shiny star. Though, I'm pretty sure she tried to get in his pants and it was a big fat N-O, so now she ignores him."

"I prefer to keep a low profile. I'll have to tell Coach not to run off at the mouth so much."

Thankfully, Hilary embarked into more of her football-party ramblings for the rest of the ride. Staring out the window, I tried to figure out how to tell King to shut the hell up.

Inside the tennis complex, I found my locker and tossed my school bag inside. Lulu dropped her shorts like she was being paid by the second, her pink thong encrusted in red crystals staring me in the face.

"Sorry 'bout that, but no shame here. We're all gonna see each other's junk soon enough."

I nodded, looking away.

How could I be so close to home, yet had never felt farther away?

CHAPTER 3

Jules

We did some core work and light weight lifting before each of us stole thirty minutes of cardio. Luckily, I was the only one who opted for the treadmill, doing a funky dance routine on the belt we did at my last school. Lulu, Hilary, the aforementioned Stacia, and a girl named Libby hit the elliptical machines like ducks in a row.

One by one, they plugged into their phones and tuned one another out while I tried to focus on the alternative music playing in the gym. I sashayed to the side for two minutes, ran backward for another two, and then walked up a hill before rinsing and repeating, only taking my eyes off the display in front of me when I was going backward.

After the workout/bonding session, I quickly showered and tried to get out of the building before being noticed.

"Hey, Jules, where you off to now?"

No such luck.

"Statistics in a bit." I mentally chided myself for not asking Hilary where she was going; I needed to fit in.

"Want a ride?" Lulu followed up behind Hilary, both of them back in their matching outfits.

"No thanks. I'm going to walk and grab a coffee."

Lord only knew, detailed dreams of the very same coach who peeked his head in during our workout kept me up late into the night.

"Why don't you give me your number so we can text you this week before workouts?"

"Um . . ." I pulled my bag higher on my shoulder, searching for the right words. "I don't have a phone, but I'll be here."

"What?"

"What did you just say?"

Their high-pitched squeals overlapped and merged into a painful shrieking in my head.

"No phone." I shrugged and turned to go.

Sensing my agitation, the others got the message and moved along, brushing past me, whispering their way toward the doors to freedom.

I leaned against the wall, trying to keep the panic at bay. I let it funnel around my ankles, but snuffed it out before it made its way up my spine.

"Jules? You okay?" a deep voice said.

I hadn't realized that my eyes were clamped shut. When they opened, there he was—the man of my dreams—his hair mussed, curling around the ears. Eyeglasses framed his face, the large, black-framed kind only models and actors could carry off.

"I'm fine. Just adjusting."

"It's going to take some time, especially after what you went through. Do you want to talk?"

My mind said no but my body said yes, forcing my head to nod.

"Come on. We'll go to my office."

I broke free from the wall and felt Coach King's hand reach for my lower back, his fingers lightly guiding me, the same ones I'd imagined to be calloused. His touch felt both right and wrong—in equal parts.

Inside his office, he said, "Have a seat. Want a drink? Water? Powerade?"

"Water, please." I gulped the cool liquid he offered me, hoping it would douse the fire raging in my belly simply from his fingers making contact with my shirt.

"How are your classes?" He sat on the edge of his desk, his arms braced on either side of him.

"I've only had one so far, but good."

"And the other girls? They're reaching out?"

Rage coiled inside me. "You didn't say anything?"

He shook his head, licking his lips, and I focused on every movement. His tongue slid across his lips, pink and slightly cracked, before it disappeared into his mouth. I felt myself mirror his actions, tasting my cherry lip gloss, wanting his lips on me.

"No," he said. "It's your story to tell. But for the record, I think you should be a little more transparent. You've overcome quite a bit. You should be proud to be back in the game."

"I'll think about it." *No way.*

"Either way, the others are being welcoming?"

"Yes, they're driving me around, filling me in on team lore."

He raised an eyebrow at that. "Do tell."

There it was again. The spark of something between us. His mouth lifted into the most delicious smile, and never before did I wish to lick something so badly.

"Apparently, you talk about me a lot. Too much. And Stacia didn't take too kindly to it."

"Stacia has . . . *had* a thing for me. But I'm a coach and she's a student, and not my type."

I focused my eyes on the floor, embarrassed by my own big mouth. Stupid girl, was I an idiot?

"That's why I'm hoping the girls are being nice to you." His voice lowered a bit, his tone turning confidential as he said, "I find it hard to be around you without crossing a line. I don't know how much of this I can do; one on one, I mean. Since I sat in your mom's kitchen, to be honest."

This time, my gaze flicked up toward his. Did he just admit what I think he did?

"What I mean is, it's frowned upon for a coach or teacher to care for a student in the way I've found myself thinking about . . . coming to care for you. Shit." He ran his hand along his forehead. "This is coming out all wrong.

You just remind me so much of me. The passion. The concentration."

I didn't know why I did it.

It could have been because it had been so long since someone genuinely cared for me other than my mom.

It could have been because I was extra vulnerable, or needed to hear something complimentary so freaking bad.

Or maybe, just maybe, I was that fucking attracted to my coach.

I pushed up from my seat, walked toward him, and ran my shaky hand along his cheek. "I know what you mean. There's a connection here. I can't put my finger on it exactly, but when I'm near you, there's something."

"It's not smart to discuss this, but hell, Jules . . . I want to."

I took a moment and stared into his eyes, seeing my reflection in his crystal-blue irises. His pupils dilated, signaling his hunger for me, and I was pretty sure mine widened as well.

For someone who felt like they'd left their ego back in California, I was surprised to find it had apparently flown back across the country.

His hand lifted and mirrored mine, running the length of my cheek and then dipping behind my neck. He tugged my hair from its messy bun and smoothed it down my back before his lips landed on mine.

"Fuck it, I can't keep my head straight when it comes to you," he murmured into my mouth.

It was gentle at first. His lips on mine, exploring and tender, then punishing. He devoured me, his tongue swiping inside my mouth. A moment later, or maybe it was hours, his lips turned gentle again as he kissed me with a closed mouth. His lips ghosted over mine, promising me more.

"I don't know what the hell is wrong with me." He tossed his glasses on the desk and they tumbled over the loose papers, clattering to a stop.

"Jules, I want you more than anything. All of you. Everything about you. More than any other woman I've ever wanted. It's a force . . . deep inside me."

I stood there silent, taking in his every syllable, warmth spreading in my veins and heat circling my heart.

"I gotta check this need at the door, but I can't shake it to save my fucking life."

He dived back in full force, his kiss rough and bruising. His lips exploded along mine, taking, giving, and making love to me in a way I'd never experienced.

But then he tore away, leaving me panting and wide-eyed as he moved behind his desk, hiding, running his hand over his forehead and scraping through his hair. All this made him even hotter.

"Christ, I don't know what overcame me. I've wanted to do that for a long time, held it at bay. I keep talking in circles. I want you, but I know I can't have you. I thought I had it in check, but clearly, I didn't. I don't." His head hung in defeat.

I moved toward him, making my way around the desk, but he backed away as I rounded the corner of it.

"Do you forgive me?" he asked. "If you want to report me . . ." His eyes blazed heat, fear, and more heat. Want and passion dueled with his anxiety over wanting me.

"I wanted it, Coach . . . King. I'm not going to report you." I plopped on the edge of his desk and took in a deep breath before letting it out with a whoosh.

Like I reminded myself daily, I was in charge these days. Always. Forever in charge. I forbade myself to allow him to take control.

"Don't . . . don't call me Coach. Doesn't seem right after what just happened. Even though it can't happen again."

"Okay, King, have it your way."

"Drew. Andrew, but mostly I'm Drew."

I watched him swallow, his Adam's apple moving up and down his throat.

"That shouldn't have happened," he said. "You already have so much on your shoulders. I'm supposed to be making your life easier."

"What if I wanted it to happen?" I shoved my hair back and twisted it into a bun again, feeling his cold, hard rejection all the way to my toes.

He hung his head, staring at the floor, his tanned hand still plunged into his hair. God, he had no idea what those actions did to me.

"It can't. It really can't."

I nodded for fear of what kind of pleading would come out of my mouth. He said he got me, understood me, gave me a second chance.

"I'm glad the girls were nice to you today," he said, still not meeting my eyes. "You should go meet up with them now. Do fun things, enjoy college life."

And like that I was dismissed from King's office and his mind.

Sadly, he was still the focal point of mine.

CHAPTER 4

Drew

ucking Christ, I swore in my head as I headed toward the men's room.
This girl was going to be the goddamn freaking death of me.

Since I lost my mind with her in my office that day, she'd spent the better part of the last month ignoring me. All I got from her was, "Yes, Coach. No problem, Coach. Of course, Coach." Just to interact with her, I found myself coming up with random shit to tell her.

Her swing was damn near perfect. She rarely lost, no matter who I put her up against. She'd just slayed the second fall tournament this past weekend, crushing everyone who came up against her. Yet I continued to bark at her.

"Adjust your grip. Widen your stance. Your shot is half a second too late."

No wonder they hated her at her last school. The other girls. Her teammates and supposed friends. It still didn't excuse what they did, but shit . . . she was amazing on the court.

And off. I wish I could tell her.

As I leaned over the sink, I squeezed my eyes shut and thought about how I was no stranger myself to shame. My mom had done a bang-up job of shaming me.

"Drew, I hope they brainwash the naughty clear out of you at prep school," my mom would say every time I went back to school. Her idea of naughty was my not agreeing to date my stepsister. Yep, my blue-blooded Southern mama saw nothing wrong with me courting my stepsister, her dumbass third husband's daughter. She wanted school to polish me up and send me home ready to acquiesce to all of her demands.

No fucking way.

The only blessing when I blew my knee out was my stepsister didn't want to talk to me anymore. I was no longer cool enough, and I was too pathetic for my mom to bother with.

She was nothing like Jules, all natural, tough on the outside but soft on the inside. Jules's hair rivaled the burned orange of the fall leaves in Ohio. Her body so long and lean, she would have given Sharapova a run for her money. I wanted to lick under and around the tiny J-shaped pendant crusted in emeralds that rested at the base of her neck, then make my way down her chest and suck on her nipples.

I bet they were pink and round and supple.

A flush spread over my face as I stared in the restroom mirror like a girl in puppy love. A white polo covered my chest, hiding the tattoos that adorned my pecs. I was hot, burning up—anger, rage, jealousy, and lust filled my veins. I needed to pull the damn shirt off, but I couldn't. I was a coach, a professional, a mentor to these young women.

Of course, now fucking Jules was playing with my head. Her attentions were focused on some asshole who played on the hoops team; Lamar, I think. The other girls were still being nice, but they didn't know her past. Her former university had sealed the case, giving Jules back all her eligibility while quietly forfeiting the rest of her old team for the season, dismissing them from the sport entirely.

It was a hush-hush case, handled even more quietly because of money and power. And Jules wanted it that way. She shouldn't have, but I could tell this one was stoic. No one was going to make an example of her unless it was about her athletic prowess.

But now she was doing what I said. Having a normal college life, and I was yanking my shit in the men's room. I turned and leaned up against the wall before pulling out my dick. I didn't give a good fuck if someone came in. I was hard as ever-loving shit, and I needed a release. Ever since the red-haired siren had touched my cheek, I was a loose cannon when it came to my dick. I wanted to use it, rough and hard—but only on her.

Let's just say, my hand wasn't calloused because of tennis anymore.

I'd made the mistake of going over to the Union for a cup of coffee and there she'd been, leaning into Lamar, close to seven feet of dark-chocolate-covered steel. Prick. Hilary was nearby with a football idiot, so all I could do was watch from afar like some lovesick teenager.

My hand pumped, my mind trying to conjure up images of Jules leaning into me like she had that ass, whispering in my ear, running the tip of her tongue along my jaw. Okay, she wasn't doing all that with Lamar. Just the leaning part, but my fucking dick wanted that and more.

My breathing quickened and I allowed myself to think about her perfect lips, plump and pink with a small mole to the left of her upper one, traveling down my chest. Her hands would open my pants, her fingers would reach in and grab me, squeeze me, admire me—*hey, I'm not small*—and then she would take me in her mouth.

And just like that, I blew my load. One image of her red hair swishing around my junk and I was a goner. Done.

Letting my head fall back against the wall, I sighed.

I needed to see her. Tell her I didn't mean what I said. I didn't want her to have a normal college experience, but she couldn't have me either.

What I really needed to do was clean my junk up.

Perhaps I should leave my coaching position.

I made most of my income managing my funds anyway. I'd survive.

CHAPTER 5

Jules

'd been spending more time on and around campus with the other girls. Hilary had even dragged me to a party or two. The first one was a basketball party in an apartment-turned-nightclub off campus. At five foot nine, I was a midget at this party. Some guy named Mel towered over a DJ table, spinning tunes, his right headphone cocked to the side while a super-tall chick talked in his ear.

Hilary bopped from random girl to random guy to another girl to another guy, kissing everyone on the cheek and saying hello, introducing me and moving on. There was some scene with a runner girl, Tingly, and a new guy on the basketball team. I had no interest in getting involved in any campus drama, so when some other dude, Lamar, introduced himself . . . I bit.

He was huge, making me crane my neck to look up at him, yet soft-spoken. Twists of braids swished around his neck as we made small talk, and he got me a diet soda and rum. He made me feel welcome, and even though there wasn't a spark in sight, I gravitated toward him.

Nothing happened, but he didn't seem to mind. I'd given him the whole *I'm not looking for anything, just got out of something ugly* speech. Maybe he'd friend-zoned me too.

Either way, after the party, we started running into each other on campus, and he made me laugh. So I started seeking him out in his usual hangouts. We were turning into good friends, even though it probably looked like more from the outside.

And so what?

King had frozen me out. Made love to my mouth and given me silent promises of more to come, and then gave me nothing. Nothing except bullshit criticism. My play was clean. He was full of it.

Last week, I'd even caught the asshole out of the corner of my eye in the Union, and I swear I didn't lean further into Lamar on purpose. Mar was already making me laugh so hard, I thought I was going to fall over— something that hadn't happened in a long, long time. But poor King looked like he wanted to slay someone. He tried to school himself over his cup of java, but I'd caught his quick jealous moment.

If he wanted me, he could have me. He still occupied most of my private moments. Hell, I'd googled the heck out of his name on the computer in the library.

But he continued to keep his distance from me.

The bad boy of tennis, he'd gone to some frou-frou tennis school in Florida before getting a full scholarship to Vanderbilt. He'd been ranked high, and despite his temper and rumors of his penchant for several seedy tattoo joints, he'd been expected to go far.

Then, the knee happened. It was his first year on the circuit after college. A slide to the side gone too far. A torn this and a torn that. Several surgeries later, and he had little lateral motion. And no more career.

I dreamed of seeing his tattoos and rubbing his knee. I wanted to sleep with the guy and care for him.

But it wasn't happening. I had to let go, which was exactly what I was lecturing myself for the thousandth time as I left the athletic complex late on Friday. I knew of several parties, but I wasn't in the mood. I was planning to watch some movies in my childhood bedroom, just relax and try to avoid my mom.

Yep.

24

"Jules," Coach King called from behind me. "Wait up."

His words came out breathy, and I'm not going to lie, I turned to some sort of goo. Teenage, boy-band goo.

I turned but stood my ground, forcing him to close the distance between us. "What?"

"I wanted to say . . . you've been playing well. Very well, and we're not even at the real season yet. I'm pleased."

When his blue eyes met mine, I raised an eyebrow. "Pleased? So I'm not hitting the ball late? Because from your comments, I thought you were anything but pleased."

He swallowed, and his Adam's apple fascinated me again. I dropped my gaze, but then his forearms caught my eye. I was screwed.

"I have to say something," he admitted. "I can't say you're perfect. For so many reasons."

I kept my gaze lowered and turned my focus on myself to keep from looking at him. My hair felt heavy on my neck, but I resisted the urge to tie it up. I felt naked in formfitting leggings and a long-sleeved T-shirt. I could see the rise and fall of my chest and the tensing of my quads.

Chancing a glance at his face, I shot back, "Oh, really? Because I already endured more than enough bullying to last me a lifetime."

He ran his fingers through his hair as he blew out a long breath. As his brow furrowed and his eyes crinkled, I wondered how old he was. Probably twenty-eight or twenty-nine, if my memory served me right.

Maybe thirty. Too young to be a coach at a major program like he was. Too young not to be playing. Too old not to have someone significant.

"I don't mean to bully you, Jules. I was thinking of the others. I don't want them to be jealous. You set the bar very high; you have to know that."

We kept a safe distance, talking like coach and athlete, even though it was late and it didn't seem like anyone was around. Everyone else had been eager to start the weekend. Maybe that was why I'd lingered so late.

"I know. I set my own standards on the court, and I don't expect anyone to keep up. That's me. I play tennis. It's all I've ever done—well, until California. There . . . I messed up everything."

"Don't be foolish. They had no right to do to you what they did. I've been around some mean pricks, and those ladies take the cake. And I use the word ladies very loosely. I'd rather say bitches."

We now stood face to face in the dim hall, each of us having inched forward. Certain as the sun had already set outside, we were about to discuss what we had never delved into before.

"Just get it out, King," I demanded.

"They shouldn't have done what they did." His face turned to stone, his expression grim.

I knew he knew, but this was different.

"They did it. Let's just say it, get it out there. Okay? You know what they did, right?" I sucked down the stale air, filling my lungs, hearing the panic crackle inside me.

"They took my phone, shoved me in the shower with some tennis boy toy, and filmed to their hearts' delight. The racquet handle up my . . . was their *pièce de résistance*. But you know what? Everyone has a guardian angel, and my old coach, the one who never told me that my shot was late, got there in time. Before they posted it. Before they shared it. So, God bless America and all that bullshit."

His reached across the small space between us and grazed his knuckles against my cheek. "Don't diminish it. You were set up by your teammates and assaulted. No one deserves that."

"I'm a better person now. Wiser. Smarter. I lay it out there. I'm up front with everyone but you. With you, I feel like a woman all over again, with desires and urges, so I push back all that crap. Maybe it's because deep down I know that you know, and yet you don't judge me. You still call my name like I'm a person. Except when you're throwing me out of your office."

His hand had found purchase on my shoulder, his thumb running circle eights that might as well have been skin to skin with the way his finger burned through the sheer fabric of my shirt.

"Another reason why I'm picking on you. I don't give a good goddamn what happened to you. I only give a damn about you. You, Jules. My feelings for you, my attraction to you is turning into a living, breathing thing. And that can't happen. Yet when I watch you play, I'm mesmerized. Haunted by your beauty and perfection." His voice lowered and became gruff, a small growl almost escaping when he added, "I want to make you all mine."

"We can be discreet," I said quickly. "I don't even own a smartphone. I live at home . . . how much damage could I do?"

I found myself bargaining with him, pleading with myself not to beg as I tried to convince myself this was all my doing. My move, my decision. All mine.

"It's not right," he said, "but I want to do that. Be discreet. Be with you."

CHAPTER 6

Drew

Jules stood before me with my hand cupping her cheek, and I was immobilized. My past tucked behind me, the future straight ahead . . . was this young woman a roadblock or the fastest route to happiness?

Be with you. I heard the words coming out of my mouth and felt my heart beating in my chest. My quads shook like I'd just played, but I hadn't done that in over five years. I was a coach, a person of authority, yet I was also a man who wanted to sleep with the woman in front of me. A woman I'd been tasked to watch over. To be careful with, gentle with, because she was fragile.

But she wasn't fragile at all. Not even one little bone in her body.

It didn't matter how many times I berated myself, I was going to have Juliette Smith. And not only once. I was going to have a lot of her.

I leaned in and placed a chaste kiss on her cheek and took her hand, leading her toward the back entrance where my car was parked. When we got to the exit, I let go of her.

"We can't be seen like this—"

She nodded, interrupting me. I wanted to do her against the steel door, but I had some self-control. Some.

I opened the door a crack and placed my hand on her lower back, guiding her into the parking lot before me and beeping the car unlocked with my free hand. The lot was lonely and dark, empty save for my black car. I swung open the passenger door before guiding her inside. Once I'd folded myself into the driver's seat, the German engine roared to life, and Dave Matthews hummed through the speakers.

"Do you feel up to coming back to my place? We can order some food."

She didn't hesitate. "Sounds great, King."

"Drew."

"King Drew with all of his demands and stipulations."

Sorry, not sorry, but my dick came to life at the sound of that nickname, and I did have some demands running through my head.

"Funny lady. I'll give you that, but Drew is fine. Maybe King later." I tossed in a wink for effect.

"Where do you live?"

There she was—straight-shooter Jules, not one bit affected by my nonsense. I knew some of her control served as an armor, but she didn't have to dig too deep. This was a strong young woman next to me.

"I bought an old farmhouse on the outskirts of town, up north. It used to belong to one of the Ag faculty at Hafton, but he died and no one in his family wanted it. It's not a working farm, but the house is pretty cool."

"Wow, I know where you mean . . . I mean, in the north. Not exactly the house. Pretty different from my suburban development."

I knew it was. I'd visited her at home.

"Yeah, it was a one-eighty from my life in South Carolina. We lived in this ridiculous mansion, complete with tennis courts and a swimming pool. And staff. My new digs are kind of rustic, and I like that."

"A Southern boy. I think I knew that."

"I went to prep school on the west coast of Florida, so I have a little honky-tonk in me from there. We'd hang with the locals any chance we could get."

"Oh yeah, your tattoos. I've read about those. Are they part of your deep, dark honky-tonk side?"

Her tone was teasing, and I wanted to throttle her with my tongue, shove it into her mouth. Yet I didn't want to quiet her. She was real. Jules didn't search for conversation or ways to compliment me. She was one hundred percent in the moment.

I could have said something cheesy like *If you're lucky, you'll get to see my tattoos.* But with Jules, I wanted to do things differently. She made me want to go about it a whole new way. It being romance, affection; the new way being . . . I hadn't a clue.

Not to mention, my cheesy come-ons would have done little for her. She wasn't a woman who was easily wooed by bullshit lines.

"At first, they were just plain old teenage rebellion, and then they were more. They were a private part of me. On my chest for me to share with who I chose."

"I get it. That's why I chose not to argue about my last school handling things privately. It was my story to share with who I felt I could share it with, and that was pretty much no one."

"I'm sorry that I even had to know what happened," I whispered. It was a sore subject; one we had skirted on more than one occasion. Sadly, I had to own up to my knowledge of it. Her old coach, Chuck, had called me himself; he believed I could be a new beginning for her.

And look what you're doing to her new fucking beginning.

I shoved any ill thoughts to the far recesses of my mind. Jules was an unstoppable force when it came to the affairs of my heart.

"When Chuck called me—he and I knew each other when I was a player—he had to explain a little about what happened to me. But that's not why I made you an offer to play. It was definitely your game tape."

"Thanks."

We sat in quiet for a few beats until I turned down my long dusty drive, the sound of my car kicking up gravel providing a change of topic. "I should probably get a truck."

"Wow, this is stunning. Look at that view."

There was a long meadow with a gazebo at the far end. My house sat to the right, pale blue clapboard with dark gray trim. I'd done some remodeling but kept it true to the era, searched the Internet for retro appliances.

"Come on, I'll show you the inside."

We walked in the front door and I watched Jules spin in her ankle boots, taking a slow three-sixty.

"I love it," she said. "It's beautiful."

"Not as much as you." And I finally took it a little cheesy.

Her laugh was deep and throaty. "You can do better than that, King."

"Yeah, I can."

I cornered her against the wall, my arms braced over her, my body not quite touching hers, and I kissed her. The moment my lips made contact with hers, a growl rumbled in my chest. She moaned in return and our hips slammed together, my hardness connecting with her heat.

Something made me stop, some last vestige of responsibility.

"Do you need to use the phone? Call home?" I mumbled the words along her lips.

What I didn't say was *I plan to keep you here a while.* I should have been ashamed, but I wasn't. Nothing had felt truer than Jules in my whole damn life.

"I should. Typically, I borrow a phone or snatch a landline somewhere."

I blew out a long breath. "You should probably block the caller ID. Not sure it will look so great having you call from my place after eight on a Friday night."

"Or any night or day," she added.

"Exactly."

"I'll block it. I already thought of that."

"It's over here." I guided her toward the kitchen with my hand on her lower back. No reason to remove it this time.

I flicked on the light and soft light flooded the room, reflecting off the yellow-enameled fridge.

"Oh my God, that's so cute. Even the phone is old-fashioned. You really are so old," she teased.

"Hey now." I pinched her cheek.

She quickly lifted the receiver and pushed the big gray buttons—*67 and then her number.

"Hey, Mom," she said softly. "I'm good. Staying out with some friends for a while. I'll be late, but I'm okay." She nodded while listening. "I will. 'Bye."

She hung up the receiver and looked at me, any remnants of the little girl in her long gone despite her having to call her mom. "She's just protective now. Wants to know I'm all right and everything. Sometimes I feel like she's worse than me."

"That's because you're a survivor, Jules. I wish I had your tenacity. When I left your kitchen last spring, that's all I kept thinking. I need to be like that girl . . . woman. When my knee blew, I was a sad fuck."

She hopped up on the kitchen island, the pots and pans dangling from above almost grazing the top of her head, and I wedged between her legs. She cupped my face in her hands and placed a gentle kiss on my mouth. It spoke volumes, but she didn't let her actions speak for her. She put her thoughts in words. This woman was brazen and bold, and I loved it.

"You deserved time to be sad. You lost your hopes and dreams. That's what you gave back to me with this position on the team."

"And we're risking it all, right this very moment." I owed her honesty in spades.

"We'll be careful. Smart. The draw is too strong."

I wasn't afraid to let my actions do the talking, so I kissed her as the last word floated from her mouth. She wrapped her legs around my waist, and we ground into each other.

"Open your eyes," I told her. "I want to see you, all of you."

Her eyes were as green as the grass in the meadow outside, and I wanted to wander in them forever.

CHAPTER 7

Jules

H e told me to keep my eyes open, and I did. I focused on the ring of blue around his pupils, so honest and clear. I saw my hunger reflected back at me in a sea of honesty.

"Let's go somewhere more comfortable, a little less industrial," he mumbled into my mouth.

We released each other's lips and he hoisted me around his waist, walking toward the back of the house. It was a ranch, and in the back was a large master bedroom with a massive king-sized poster bed situated in the middle.

He set me down gently and knelt on the floor, taking off my boots before sliding his hands up my legs. He grasped my leggings and drew them down, retracing his steps for my underwear. When they were gone as well, I was spread open, glistening in front of him. He stood and tugged his shirt over his head, tossing it on the floor.

And there are the famous tattoos.

He didn't waste any time, kicking off his shoes and shucking off his pants. *Commando, yep. And wow. Large.*

He leaned over me, and the tip of his erection grazed my thigh. "One more thing." He pulled my shirt over my head and made quick work of my bra.

And then he was on me.

He held his weight up on one elbow while he placed a trail of kisses over my collarbone, across my breast, and back to my nipple. There, he sucked on one while he toyed with the other. I squirmed, aiming for contact in the middle. His tip moved over my most sensitive spot, and I was so close to exploding, I had to bite down on my tongue.

His free hand left my nipple to move down and trace my wetness before he slipped a finger inside. His mouth moved to my other nipple, laving and loving.

My hands ran down his back while my eyes wandered his chest. A scorpion lay over his heart, a snake ran the length of his abs, and a crest covered his left pec.

I brought one hand to his chest and traced the scorpion. "That's pretty evil," I said on a moan as he slipped another finger inside me.

"It was there to protect my heart from the ill intentions of my family," he mumbled. "More on that later."

His lips wrapped around my nipple and his fingers swirled on my most sensitive spot, and that was it. I exploded. My eyes finally snapped closed in ecstasy, Drew the only word in my language.

He caressed me through the wave, slowing when I slowed, reading my body like a court in a doubles game.

"All that from just my hand . . . Wonder what will happen when I get to use my mouth?" He chuckled as he shifted, running his length against my quivering heat.

"How about you finally get inside me?"

"Ready?" His voice was hoarse, his eyes mere slits, filled with passion and heat.

When I nodded, he reached to the nightstand and grabbed protection, tearing the package open with his teeth.

"King Drew." As I taunted him, he continued to tease me, rubbing himself along me, but never entering.

"Yes, Miss Juliette?"

34

"I want you."

"Then you shall have me."

He entered me with one push, long and deep, sucking in a breath before withdrawing and settling into an easy pace with languid thrusts.

I hooked a leg on his hip and he sped up, each time a little faster and harder, hitting just the spot. Like a fool in love, I went off again. I felt myself tightening around him and then he was with me, groaning and emptying into the condom.

CHAPTER 8

Drew

lifted her up and snatched back the covers, drawing them over us before plopping down and pulling her against me.

Snatching my cell phone off the nightstand, I asked her, "Pizza? That's about all we get out here, and it takes a while."

"Sounds good. I'm a vegetarian, though."

"No prob. One Meat Lovers Supreme coming up."

My hand drifted down and pinched her butt. It felt natural and familiar, this lying here with her. But it wasn't.

I murmured our order to the teen on the line and went back to cuddling with Jules.

We made out leisurely—as if we had all the time in the world—and I got to see what happened when I used my mouth.

And when she used hers, I teased her that she wasn't truly a vegetarian.

When the doorbell rang, I told her to stay put. Tossing on a pair of shorts, I grabbed the pizza and brought it back to bed. We ate it straight from the box, laughing and teasing.

Yep, I definitely hadn't been thinking straight when I got involved with my player, but could anything have stopped me?

Doubtful.

Even as I drove her home, stopping a few houses away from hers to drop her off and then watch her walk back to her childhood home, there was little I could do to convince myself that I didn't want her.

The next few weeks found me sinking deeper and deeper into this secret relationship with Jules. I rode her like a stallion at practice, kicking and prodding her to be better. And later, I did much the same in bed. My gut pinched every time I heard her make excuses to the team and her mom about where she was going, lying so she could be with me.

On the nights I didn't see Jules, I worried myself to sleep over how this could continue into the season. Then I would wake up in a cold sweat over it ending.

We had one more late fall tournament before the holidays began, and then after winter break, the season would kick in. The day before we were supposed to travel to Pennsylvania to play an Ivy League squad, I walked into the Union, the weight of the world riding my shoulders. Some people had a debt monkey; I had my own personal guilt monkey.

I needed caffeine and sugar to wake me the fuck up. Jules had come over the night before and slipped off her coat, revealing she was wearing her tennis whites. Except with nothing underneath. Her nipples plucked through her see-through white tank, and when she bent over to place her coat on the couch . . . *oh fuck*, stars flooded my eyes.

There was her ass on full display, smooth and creamy, and a hint of promise between her legs. I slid right down behind her and took advantage of her being bare. My dick harder than it had ever been, I worshipped her, right there in my living room, my bad knee bent on the hardwood floor.

I'd eaten her up, swallowed her release as her screams imprinted on my heart. "Drew, Drew," was forever marked in my brain. When her breathing slowed, I climbed back up her body and bent her over the sofa and had my way with her . . . before having to take her home.

I hadn't slept at all afterward. My heart was twisted in knots, and my brain was even worse.

So when I swept through the Union and glimpsed Jules in the corner with Hilary and Lulu, surrounded by ten guys, all athletes, all of them with eyes on my woman . . . I went nuts. Lamar had his usual perch right next to Jules, and she was laughing, fucking sparkling at something he'd just said.

She didn't see it, but she was a gem. My gem.

I wanted to roar; I wanted to punch something, someone. I was so caught up in my caveman fantasy, I didn't realize I'd walked into someone until hot coffee soaked the front of my shirt.

"Shit," I muttered, suddenly remembering I was a coach and at the university where I worked.

"Dude, you fucking walked straight into me!" some young thing yelled at me.

Hell, they were all young things, except for Jules.

"I'm sorry, I'll get you another," I said in a low voice, not wanting to draw any unnecessary attention.

But Jules had seen me. Green eyes bore into me from the other side of the Union, and I could feel their heat and disappointment. She needed to keep up appearances, and it was me who wasn't helping.

Yanking my wallet out of my back pocket, I tossed a ten at the girl and escaped out the back door.

CHAPTER 9

Jules

O
h no, he wasn't getting away with that bullshit. I excused myself
from the table, claiming my mom wanted to see me this afternoon,
and ran out the front of the building. Ducking to the left, I made my
way around the back and off to the athletic complex.

Fucker. He wasn't allowed to stalk me like that.

I had to appear normal, even though I was screwing the coach. He needed
to put up a normal front too.

Inside the building, I went straight to his office and found him stewing
at his desk. His head was buried in his hands with his elbows planted on the
desk, putting those sexy forearms on display.

"King?" When I saw him hurting, the irritation and rage fled my body.
All I wanted to do was comfort him.

"I'm sorry, Jules," he said in a hoarse whisper, and his next words were
softer, barely audible. "I freaked."

I walked in and shut the door, then locked it behind me. "None of them
mean anything to me."

"I don't like this. I want us to be out in the open. You and me on a

39

restaurant date, not Chinese takeout or pizza delivery, hiding at my house. You deserve hand holding and PDA. This is wrong."

"Don't," I begged, my entire body going tense at the fear of where this was going.

"It's wrong, and I take all the responsibility."

I shook my head and walked around the desk, taking in his dark-washed jeans and rumpled hair. His Henley tugged and pulled around his biceps; his head hung low as he pulled on the back of his neck.

I sat in his lap and kissed his cheek. "I'm yours," I said into his ear before biting his lobe.

Apparently, I didn't need to say any more, because he picked me up and laid me out on his desk. Within seconds, my shoes were off, my pants on the floor, and my shirt over my head.

I whispered, "King Drew," and he growled in return. One finger was inside me, then two, readying me, but I didn't need it. I was always ready for him.

His mouth was on my nipple, his hand pumping into me, the light shift of the desk humming around us. I banged the back of my head on the desk as my climax hit me, and my back arched. It didn't matter—I felt too good to care.

And then he was in me, fast and deep, his movements desperate, urgent. He was also bare, but I didn't say anything. Drew was in some kind of state, determined to mark me and make me his. He didn't realize he already had.

Something amazing built inside me, then exploded as he stiffened, pumping his feelings into me. We kissed, our tongues dueling, swallowing each other's cries of ecstasy.

And then came the knock.

"Coach, it's Stacia. Are you here?"

CHAPTER 10

Jules

We got a lucky break yesterday—I'd hidden under the desk while Drew threw his clothes back on. He pretended to be leaving and cut Stacia off at the door, asking her, "What's up?" while pulling it closed behind him.

After I heard their footsteps retreat, I came out from under the desk and slipped on my clothes. Then I snuck out, looking both ways before leaving the building.

Now as I made my way around Hafton's campus, my bike tires crunching along the fallen leaves as I pedaled to the athletic complex, I knew we had to be more careful.

As I said good-bye to my mom that morning, I promised myself to do better, to watch my back and King's. She was off to her job in the registrar's office, and I was on my way to Psych. My teammates hadn't been in class, which was why I headed to the complex as soon as class was dismissed. Something was up, and I hoped like hell it had nothing to do with me.

The heavy door banged behind me, and before I even made it twenty feet, Lulu came running up to me.

"Shit, Jules, we didn't know how the hell to reach you. Thank God you're here. Emergency meeting in the weight room. Now."

She pulled me down the hall and into the bright lights of the gym. Everyone was seated on various weight benches, their legs stretched out in front of them, a mishmash of leggings and skinny jeans. I sat on an empty bench and pulled my legs under me Indian-style.

Crisscross applesauce, my old teacher used to say.

There were whispers and hushed speculation, but no one stared at me or mentioned my name. Whispered snatches of *King, breakdown, too young* floated around me.

"Morning, ladies." The athletic director walked into the complex with a tall bald guy on his right. "Thank you for getting together on such short notice. As of last evening, Coach King resigned. It seems that the coaching job was too much for him at this time. We were lucky to be able to bring Coach Hall out of retirement for this season while we look for a replacement."

A chorus of *What? Why? What the heck?* filled the room.

"I know it's a disappointment. You all did very well with Coach King over the last two years, and he worked hard to get the team where it is, but Hall is a longtime Hafton coach and employee, and a devoted fan. He will do right by you. And now I'll leave him to discuss the schedule with you."

I didn't hear a word of what Hall said. He rambled about the season coming upon us quickly, January, mandatory practices, and optional workouts.

My head spun. King was gone.

He didn't say good-bye. Not that he could have called my house and said to my mom, "Excuse me, Mrs. Smith, but I've been sleeping with your daughter and now I'm running away, so . . ."

Maybe he was still at his house? If I had a phone, I could Uber there. But I didn't.

Fucking crap, my mom and her stupid plan to erase what happened by sheltering me from any further scandals by keeping me unplugged. She would absolutely shit if she knew what happened this go-round.

I'd have to come up with an excuse. Borrow her car and go to his house. *Now.*

I grabbed my stomach and pretended to be sick. Actually, I full-on felt sick. I was having some bad reaction to Drew disappearing.

"I'm sorry, Coach Hall. I'm not feeling well."

"You're excused," he said, his tone all business.

His voice didn't make my legs shake; his eyes didn't make me feel weak in the knees.

I wanted King back.

Despite my insistence to my mom in the beginning of the year to keep her distance from me at school and give me space, I rushed to the registrar's office. She was surprised to see me, and my stomach clenched as I lied to her, made up a story about a fellow player needing to get to a doctor's appointment, and how I volunteered.

"I need to borrow your car," I asked quietly.

"I'm so glad you're making friends," she said.

If she only knew.

Then I rushed to his house, taking the turns that had been committed to memory from riding beside him. When I pulled up in front, I blanched at the sight of the FOR SALE sign in his front yard and the U-Haul parked around back. The front door was open and King walked through it, carrying out a box.

When I got out and slammed the door on my mom's sedan, he looked up, shock and fear on his face.

"Jules, you shouldn't be here," he said sternly, his brow furrowed.

"Why? You changed your mind?" I felt some psycho *Basic Instinct* boil-the-bunny shit flowing through my veins.

"No," he said quietly, setting down the box he was holding before walking toward me. "I want what's best for you, and this isn't it."

"You don't get to decide that." My words were steady as I planted my feet in his driveway and stood firm, refusing to move an inch.

"I do. One scandal was enough for you. You don't need this. Or me."

He leaned forward and his lips touched mine in a closed-mouth kiss, full of regret but no fire, as his arm slid around my back and pulled me tight. It was a good-bye kiss, no doubt about it.

I felt his hard abs, the beginning of an erection, and his rapid heartbeat. It was thumping so hard and fast, it felt like it was going to leap out of his chest. How could he think this was wrong? That *we* were wrong?

He pulled back slightly and rested his forehead against mine. I sensed him breathe me in as he ran his nose along my hairline, and I wrapped my arms around his waist.

I clutched him tightly like a toy on Christmas morning. I wasn't going to let him go.

"I have to go, Jules. This isn't going to end well for either of us, and I want . . . I *need* it to end well for you."

I shook my head, a croak dislodging from my throat, but my words caught there just the same.

"Yesterday, with Stacia . . . we could have been caught. We can be caught anytime. It's wrong. It's my fault, so I'm leaving."

"I don't want you to," I pleaded, realizing my control was all gone. It had slipped through my fingers, and I didn't care.

"I am. I have to."

"Where are you going? This is all happening so fast."

He moved away and opened my car door, his expression begging me to get in. "It's not for you to know. Coach Hall will keep me updated on the team. It needs to be this way."

I shook my head again, tears coming this time, washing away what little makeup I wore and dripping onto my shirt.

"There's no use denying how much I've come to care for you, Jules, but you have to leave now. I need to go. It's all for the best."

He practically lifted me and put me back in the driver's seat of my mom's car. His hand brushed gently over my cheek, moving a few damp strands of hair from my face.

"Good-bye, Jules."

The door closed and the locks engaged, cutting through me like a knife.

44

CHAPTER 10.5

Jules

For weeks, I dragged my tired ass around, pretending everything was A-OK. I became convinced if I didn't let on about our relationship, Drew would come back. He'd see everything was fine and nice.

But, really, toast was nice. I was more like a burned piece of toast to be discarded. Garbage. Rubbish.

When I finally lay my head down on my pillow every night, I felt defeated.

I was the ultimate idiot. First, the victim of a stupid sex crime. Helpless and needy, to boot.

Then I'd fallen for the man in charge, my coach. He'd been the smart one to escape. And fast, at that.

After he left, three or four weeks passed where I barely slept at all. Eventually, my body became cloaked in pure exhaustion.

At least, I'd thought that's what it was.

Then all of a sudden, sleep started coming easily to me. In class. In bed. In the Union Building.

That whole time, my only salvation was tennis. I took out my frustrations on the ball, beating the hell out of it, harder and harder.

"Turn it down a tiny bit, Juliette," Coach Hall called to me. "We don't need you killing Stacia during a practice. Add more precision and less animosity, Juliette. You're going to tear the yellow right off the ball."

I didn't even bother to correct him on my name.

Jules had become reserved for Drew, and only Drew. I'd even put my green *J* in the bottom of my underwear drawer. The way he'd licked around it, his tongue pushing it out of the way as he sucked on my neck . . . he owned the damn necklace too. My mom had given it to me when I received my first tennis scholarship—the last time she'd really been proud of me.

"Jesus, girl, you look flushed," Stacia said to me after our practice match. "Coach told you to slow it. I mean, I can take it, but holy shit, you're on some sort of vendetta lately."

"Just my competitive spirit," I said before I guzzled some water.

"God, I can see your pulse racing in your neck. Sit down," she ordered.

Quite frankly, I hated that she was taking an interest in me. It felt forced, even though it really wasn't. It was just my past experiences rearing their ugly head. But honestly, it felt like my heart was going to gallop out of my chest, so I listened.

When I sat down, Lulu plopped down next to me.

"You good?" she asked.

"Yeah, I think I just went a little crazy out there."

"I saw. I mean, are you *good* good? Hilary said you were hanging out with Lamar a lot, and now no one sees you except for at practice and class. Something happen with him? I know you keep to yourself and all that, but if you need to talk . . ."

When I laughed, water bubbled back up my throat. "No, nothing happened with Lamar."

"Again, we're here for you. I know you're private, but if you need to talk, I can be discreet—"

"All good," I said quickly, cutting her off. "I swear." No one had ever been there for me before—until Drew—and look where that got me.

Taking another sip of water, I was surprised when it suddenly came back up faster than it went down, and I threw up all over my shoes.

Lulu stood up and took my hand. "I'm not arguing with you anymore,

Jules. We're going to the health center. You look like shit."

Our fingers woven together, her feet leading the way—it was like soup for the soul. Until we got to the health center and they ran my labs.

When I got the results, Lulu jumped to conclusions, Lamar being the unlucky target of her suspicions. Hilary ran to the health center after getting a text from Lulu, and threatened to call Lamar and let him in on what he'd done. Which I kept trying to explain was nothing.

The one saving grace was that Stacia was too busy to come with us.

When I quit the team shortly afterward and left school, claiming I wasn't interested in tennis anymore and therefore couldn't keep my scholarship, Lulu and Hilary were the only ones wise enough to know I was lying. But they were still convinced Lamar was the guilty party.

Thanks to some unofficial sister code I'd never heard of, they promised to never reveal my secret. With kisses and hugs and belly rubs, we said good-bye, promising to stay in touch.

Sadly, I didn't plan to keep my end of the deal. When it was over, it was over.

Wasn't that what Drew had shown me?

CHAPTER 11

Jules

As soon as I'd come clean to my mom about my condition, she wrote me off as a great big failure. It was my mission to prove her wrong. Things didn't exactly work out as planned, but I did my best. I owed it to someone else to be the very best I could be.

On a promise and a prayer, I'd headed toward North Carolina. I found a job teaching tennis at a tennis club, and transferred my credits to a small community college there.

That was seven years and a lifetime ago. College and tennis were both long behind me, but not the memories of King. Leaving those behind was a physical impossibility for me.

Most nights when I lay down, I tried not to dwell on the day it all changed. I forced myself not to think about that day, about turning the key in the ignition or putting the car in drive. I wouldn't think about King's devastated face growing smaller and smaller until only his silhouette haunted me in the rearview mirror, a face I still saw sometimes in my dreams, and daily when I looked at her. Except hers was framed with strawberry-blond hair, alight with the exact big blue eyes I dreamed of.

Speaking of, I checked the rearview mirror as I drove along the highway, leaving North Carolina behind. It was time for a new beginning for me . . . and for the precious six-year-old girl asleep in the backseat.

PART TWO

CHAPTER 12

Drew

I ran my hand through my hair, which was shorter these days, and swiped the sweat from my brow. Sighing, I tried not to roll my eyes at the overeager girl on the treadmill next to me.

"I've never seen you here before," she purred, but it came out as more of a scream as she spoke over the music piping through her neon-pink earbuds.

Forget it, girl. She was a freaking baby, and I was a grown man immune to silly come-ons.

Most of the time.

"I'm here every morning at six," I said matter-of-factly, barely breathing heavily even though I was on my third mile. "Except Sundays when I sleep in, and I'm here at seven."

It was the truth, and everyone at Extreme Fit knew it. If I missed a day, they'd probably send an ambulance to my house. I was a fixture at the gym, every single morning, every damn day.

"Oh, that's awesome." She plucked the bud from her ear closest to me, and I couldn't help but notice her matching neon-pink nails. "I have a new schedule, and I'm trying to come in before my nine a.m. class." She revealed bright white teeth in a wide smile, her blond ponytail swinging from side to side as she ran.

Most men would have bitten—asked for her number and banged her a few days later. She was young, hot, and obviously willing.

But not me.

I nodded and focused on the TV above me—*SportsCenter* repeating the same loop I'd already seen.

If she were a redhead? Maybe.

Look, I wasn't meant to be celibate, so every now and again, I found a redhead who happened to be pleasing to the eye. They were never as satisfying as I'd hoped, and they always left me wanting more.

Not with them, though. With someone else I'd left in my past.

It had been my own doing, the leaving part. Something I needed to regularly remind myself.

Oblivious to my disinterest, the blonde rattled on. "I'm a pre-med major, so my classes are early. They like to get us used to being up early."

Of course, after I realized my mistake, I'd tried to look for her—Jules—wanting to keep tabs on her. I had called Coach Hall and asked after the team, how they were doing and shit. I'd even snagged the roster off the Internet, but she wasn't on it. A few times a week, alone in my office, I would google her name.

Nothing. I never found a damn crumb.

"What do you do?"

I snagged my towel off the machine and wiped around my neck, slowing my stride. "Sorry, I don't mean to be rude, but I gotta roll. I work in finance, so that's why I have to get in here and get done early."

It was mostly a lie. After running my investment firm by myself for a year, I added a sizable number of associates and a few junior partners. If I wanted to go in late now, I could.

I'd always had a knack for watching the market and picking funds. It didn't take me long to get my broker's license after leaving Ohio. With a black book full of old prep school contacts, it took even less time to fill my client roster.

After a proven track record in the first year, they all sent me their newer, richer friends. It was like a pyramid scheme for high rollers.

"Good luck to you," I said to the young chippie as I wiped down my machine.

"Thanks. Do you—"

She'd started to say something else, but I was already gone.

My day had officially gone to shit.

Seated behind my oversized desk, I leaned back and listened to Sully on my cell phone.

For just a second, I put my cell on mute and called my assistant on the landline. "Hey, Shelby, can you call my two o'clock and let them know I'm running fifteen minutes late?"

With my full attention back on my client and friend, I unmuted my cell and said, "Yeah, I hear you, Sully. Either way, this fund isn't going to do you wrong, and if it performs the way they're thinking, you'll be able to retire sooner rather than later."

"What the hell would I do if I retired?"

I tossed my glasses on my desk and propped my Pumas on top of all the papers. It was business casual at my place every day. I didn't have time for suits or ties, or any of that nonsense. My loneliness did just fine strangling me.

"Let's see . . . You could play eighteen holes every day, lose the gut—"

He laughed into the phone. "Hey now." He let out a long sigh and pretended to be thinking about my recommendation. "Yeah, buy the riskier one. My golf clubs are calling to me as we speak. But when Rosie is good and pissed at me, I'm telling her you made me do it."

I closed my eyes. I didn't know what it was like to have someone want me to slow down and spend time with her.

"Blame me all you want. The ladies all love me, Sull."

"You should find one of your own, Drew. One to keep."

"Hey, I'm already running late for my next meeting. I'll have Shelby send you the papers to sign for the buy-in."

"Yeah, right." Sully let me off the hook, but not without a huff.

I wasn't getting a girl of my own, because the only girl I wanted was now a grown woman who had probably long forgotten about me.

My mood dampened, I tramped out into the Florida heat and off to the coffee place down the street for my meeting.

CHAPTER 13

Jules

"Mom, I don't want to eat breakfast!"

"Darla, you have to eat something." It was an ongoing battle, and one I was determined to win.

She shook her head at me and stuck out her lower lip. I guzzled half a cup of coffee, hoping to chase away the aftereffects of a late night and regain my composure.

"Come on, honey. Just a little cereal, or how about some toast? Gotta feed your brain."

"Fruit Loops?" Her smile turned into a smirk, transforming her into a little-girl version of her father and guaranteeing her the win.

"Sure."

After insisting she was starting first grade today and therefore was a big girl, Darla slopped the milk in the bowl under my watchful eye. She could pour her own milk. *Sort of.*

Pretending not to notice the sticky mess on the counter, I reminded her, "Your teacher is Ms. Green. She's supposedly very nice. Be good today, Dar."

She nodded, stuffing her cheeks full of food coloring, sugar, and corn-syrupy carbs.

"Good?"

She nodded again, then swallowed. "Do you think I'm going to have a birthday party? I know it was last month, but maybe?"

I reached across the counter and swiped her strawberry-blond bangs out of her blue eyes. Her DNA was mostly her dad's—olive skin, light hair, and eyes as deep as the Mediterranean. Smirk and all, I loved every inch of her, but there were moments I wanted to run away.

Like now.

"I know we didn't have one for you—yet—but we will. We were moving, remember, and I thought you'd want to meet some new friends . . ." *And money was tight.*

I didn't say the last part; she didn't need to know that. It wasn't her fault. Yeah, I'd never finished college because of my daughter, but getting knocked up was all on me. I knew the risk when I had sex without a condom, and I didn't care in that moment.

Darla blinked, and her bangs caught her long eyelashes again. "Maybe I can have a pajama party like in the book we read last night?"

"Sure, baby. You behave at school and we'll plan it. I know everyone is going to love you, and you'll probably have a huge guest list by the end of the week." I did my best to reassure her, figuring it was nerves over making friends or going to a new school causing her to focus on the party.

"Done!" She jumped up and grabbed her backpack.

"Let's go."

I placed the bowl in the sink and grabbed my keys after refilling my mug. I'd tossed on running shorts and a T-shirt to wear for walking Darla to the bus. My plan was to take a quick run afterward, and then a short rest before grocery shopping and paying bills, all before my little girl got home from school. Then I could spend some actual time with her. I was off on Monday nights, and I couldn't wait to be home with Darla instead of relying on the babysitter, Molly, to put her to bed.

We walked down the steps and to the corner, Darla talking the whole way about her upcoming pajama party.

"Popcorn and the minion movie. And pancakes! Oh, I'll need new jammies," she said, chattering on about all her plans for her party.

For six, she was something. Smart, funny, and wise. Sometimes I worried she was too wise, having only one parent.

But I did the best I could.

The week flew by. As predicted, Darla had ten girls on her list and fifty outlandish requests for the party. She wanted a sleepover, a purple-and-pink cake, sparkly streamers, hot cocoa with pink marshmallows at bedtime, and strawberry milk and chocolate chip pancakes in the morning.

"And maybe Ms. Green could stop by?" she asked Saturday night as I got ready for work, right before I made an epic mistake.

On her actual birthday, I'd given her a manicure and pedicure at home, applying some brand-new neon-green sparkly polish while she sat curled up in my robe. I should have left it at that.

Nope, tonight I screwed up and asked what she wanted for a *real* gift as I secured my cranberry-red tie into place before a long night of waiting tables.

"I want a dad," she said. "My dad. Maybe he'll feel bad he missed my birthday and come?" Her voice started out vibrant and strong, only to be swallowed up with the threat of tears.

She'd jabbered about her dad from time to time. I never had the heart to let her know he didn't even know she existed.

Sucking in a deep breath, I steadied my voice before I spoke. "He loved you very much, but he couldn't stay with us. It happens sometimes to mommies and daddies. I'm sure he thinks about you all the time," I said, reassuring her with the same sentiment I always did.

It was vague and stupid and wrong, but it was all I could muster. Saying the truth out loud hurt me too much, and I had to have some sense of self-preservation.

To my shame, I never even gave Drew a chance . . . right away, I'd written him off. I'd deliberately made myself hard to be found, and I never tried to seek him out. In my heart, I knew he would have done right by us, but I was selfish. I wanted him to do right by *me*.

He might have changed his mind, given us a chance, but that didn't negate him deserting me. It was immature of me to focus on that, but I was a victim of my heart.

Staring into Darla's hopeful blue eyes, ones just like his, I almost felt like trying to find him.

But what if he rejected me? What if he'd made a life and moved on? Had other children with another woman?

The fact was, it wasn't only me who would be affected if I found him. Both of us would. We were a package—Darla and me—a pair, a team, a double.

During my shift later that night, I swore in my head, unable to push the memory of her tears aside. *Fuck*, now I was forced to wait tables for Florida's finest with the bruising memory of a pained and hurting Darla weighing on me.

Don't judge. I was miserable.

"Claire?"

My floor manager stole me from my painful thoughts, calling me by my middle name, which I'd assumed full time. It was the only name Bryce had ever known for me, and we'd come to Florida from the Southern Steak and Sea's North Carolina franchise together. We'd worked together for six years, ever since I'd shown up for an interview with a month-old Darla in tow.

"What's up, Bryce?" I leaned my hip against the kitchen counter, keeping one eye on deck in case my latest order surfaced.

"Jenny was supposed to help with the dinner in the private room, but she went home sick."

I shook my head. "You know I hate the back room. Hated working it in North Carolina, and I'm sure it's worse here. It's always a bunch of guys getting grabby because the doors are closed, or a room full of gray-hairs who don't tip shit . . . think their steak was overpriced and the creamed corn not creamy enough. Nope."

"Come on, Claire. I need someone good. It's a big corporate dinner, so they'll tip. And I'll put Paul back there as a runner or busser, so no grabbing."

"I'm new here. Trying to get to know the weekend regulars. I need the tip money."

"I'll owe you. No lunches on your schedule for a week or two. Fridays and Saturdays in the best sections. Please? I don't know the other servers well enough to trust them with a party of thirty."

The bell dinged, and the guy in whites bellowed my name.

"Claire!"

Before I could react, Bryce took over. "Paul, why don't you run this food out for Claire and then follow her to the private dining room."

"I didn't even agree," I said to Bryce, pretending to pout. He knew I'd give in.

"This is the last ticket you have open before the second seating, so I'll have Stella take care of desserts and checks."

"No lunches for a while," I called after Bryce, tightening my bun and sticking my pen behind my ear. Cracking my neck from side to side, I straightened my tie and smoothed my white shirt before heading to the back.

Bracing my shoulder against the heavy wooden door, I pushed into the back room. The smell of crisp money and wood paneling engulfed me.

I hated everything about the back room, including the name. It intimated exactly what the men thought they might find there. Perhaps I despised it because it reeked of *man* and reminded me of what I didn't have, and now there were close to thirty of them milling around the bar in the far corner.

With tumblers of whiskey in their hands and the scent of a decent cigar in the air, the men laughed as they stood around and made small talk. No one was seated yet, so I turned toward the door, deciding to sneak out for another fifteen minutes to try to pry myself out of my self-imposed funk.

Only two steps away from freedom, the sound of a deep chuckle made goose bumps rise over my entire body. The glorious sound rumbled through the room, taking hold of my heart like it had so many years ago.

Shocked, I stumbled and reached out and braced myself on the oak-paneled wall to keep from falling. I begged myself not to turn around, but then I heard it again. Like when a favorite song comes on in the car as you park at home and you can't bear to get out of the car, I stood with my back to the room and my ears perked up for my most favorite song ever.

I could only make out murmurs rather than actual words, but since I'd heard the laugh, I knew which murmurs were his—full-bodied like an aged Scotch, smooth like silk with a touch of gruff, and just right. His laugh rang out again, and it stabbed at my heart. He was happy and good, had probably made a life for himself as I'd suspected. A better life than he could have had being saddled with me.

Desperately, I wanted to turn to see if the crinkles around his eyes had deepened. More than anything in this world other than Darla's safety, I wanted to look. Just a quick glance.

But I didn't. My damn need for self-preservation kept my eyes trained on the oak paneling in front of me. I panicked, needing to get the hell out of here and tell the boss I didn't feel well.

I needed to move.

Again.

To Alaska.

He'd lived in Florida once long ago—on the other coast, the honky-tonk part. I had no idea why I'd never considered he'd be here. On the east coast. At my steak place. My refuge.

He'd loved that old farmhouse, so I always imagined he'd found another. A clapboard mansion filled with kids and a beautiful wife, somewhere quiet and serene.

It was a foolish notion. He was a bad boy from way back when.

"Oh, hey! Ma'am, can we get some crab cakes and shrimp?" some asshole bellowed at my back.

Ma'am? I'm a ma'am? No way. Freaking back room.

I ran my hand along my forehead, pushing back nonexistent stray hairs, and out of habit, tightened my bun. It wasn't messy anymore. These days, I wore it low and perfectly round, like my carefully constructed persona.

I tried to make myself nod, confirming the shrimp, and leave.

"I'm sorry, did you hear me?" the same ass grumbled.

This was exactly why I hated working the private room. It was always a bunch of entitled pricks.

My head twisted to my right where the asshole's comments came from. I only turned partway and was about to speak, but there he was, Drew King, standing next to a heavyset man. The one I presumed to be the mouthy jerk.

Drew stood tall, more tanned than I remember. His hair was cropped shorter and maybe was a shade darker, and light stubble covered his chin. Yes, his eyes were still as blue as the sea, and they stared back at me.

I looked around the room in an effort to control my growing panic. Surely everyone saw me drowning, yet no one tossed me a life preserver.

My brain screamed *Help! Run!* but my heart nailed my feet to the floor, making it impossible to move an inch.

"Sully, seriously," he said to his friend, "it's not necessary. She's obviously waiting for us to finish our drinks."

I thought that's what I heard him say, I couldn't be sure. My heartbeat was pounding in my ears, and my lungs didn't want to work.

"No, you're right. I can grab you the appetizers," I finally choked out. As quickly as I could, I turned and began to push open the door.

Where the hell is Paul?

A burning fire broke out on my shoulder. No, not a fire, it was Drew's hand singeing me through my shirt, straight to the bone.

I wanted to yell for water, for a fire extinguisher, but that would have been too literal. I knew the burning was coming from inside. My heart was engulfed in flames.

"Jules?" He held me still, his fingers gripping my shoulder almost painfully. "What is this? A joke?"

He gestured with his free hand, indicating my black slacks, and then flicked at my tie.

"What the fuck?" The last part was a whisper, his eyes nasty and violent, a storm brewing deep behind his dilated pupils.

How could this be happening? I'd made a life, a lonely one, but a life. He loved the farmhouse and the west coast of Florida. Why was he in my restaurant? Here in my little bubble where I served the wealthy so I could raise my daughter—by myself.

Without him.

"Claire? You good?" Paul said as he finally showed up. "I'm sorry, one of the steaks I delivered for your table wasn't the right temperature and I had to run it back."

"Who's Claire? You're not Juliette Smith? I could've sworn you looked just like her." Confused, Drew frowned at me, his brow furrowing as his eyes searched mine.

Maybe I can pull it off? I thought, but that was stupid. That was the kind of immature thinking that came from exiling myself, from running away and refusing to keep up with the times and with social media.

"Same eyes, green as the grass. Red hair. And those lips," Drew murmured to himself.

If I didn't know him and all that we'd been through, I would've taken him for a crazy person.

Paul finally grew some balls. "Excuse me, but would you mind removing your hand from her?"

Drew released his grip on me and looked deeper into my eyes, maybe even into my soul. "Jules? I know that's you. Aren't you a vegetarian? What in the hell are you doing working in a steak place?"

I think I nodded. Twice. Or maybe it was one really long nod.

"Paul, I'm not feeling so . . . hot. Excuse me," I said, and I ran.

CHAPTER 14

Drew

Christ! What just happened?

Who the hell is Claire? What the ever-loving fuck is going on?

And what happened to my Jules?

My mind raced as I stood stock-still, watching the redheaded waitress run away from me.

Move.

My body finally complied and started making its way to the side door I'd seen Claire escape through.

"Claire!" I called after the slender figure about to dodge into some sort of break room.

"Hey," another dude called after me. The maître d', or whoever the fuck he thought he was. "You can't go back there."

"Sorry, I really needed to catch up with Claire. She's an old friend." I turned and put on a smile.

"Holy shit. You—" He said it on a whisper and was about to say something else when Claire interrupted him.

"Bryce, don't. Leave it," she warned from the doorway.

Don't what? Leave what? What the hell did all that mean?

"Claire, you want to clue me in?" This came from Bryce, the tall, buff asshole now standing between Jules and me.

"Bryce, it's okay. I'm just going to clear up some confusion, and then I need to go home. I'm sorry. I feel like crap. I'll make it up to you and work lunches."

"Stop it, Claire. You're not working lunches. You know that, but I need you to tell me you're okay."

"She's fine, buddy." I couldn't watch the conversation volleying between these two anymore. It was my turn.

"I didn't ask you," he spit out. "I asked her. Claire?"

Her name's Juliette, you ass. Jules to me.

"I'm good, Bryce," she said, and held up a hand. "Thank you."

Frowning, Bryce said, "I'll be right down the hall."

"You do that, Bryce," I said snidely, unable to help myself.

"Drew," she said, my name rolling off her lips sending shock waves down my spine. She shook her head at me. "Don't. He's my boss."

"Sorry, dude."

Bryce didn't even acknowledge my apology. "Why don't you go in there?" He nodded toward the break room.

She nodded, and I moved forward faster than a lob during a match point. I shut the door behind us, the click of the lock loud in the awkward silence.

"Jules, what are you doing here?"

She leaned against the far wall and released her bun, allowing her hair to cascade over her shoulders. "Working. What does it look like?"

"What's with the Claire thing?" I kept my distance, sensing my nearness was not welcome.

"It's my middle name. What I go by these days. Jules was then, and Claire is now."

"Why?" My hand twitched to brush the long layers away from her eyes.

"It was for the best. To make a new life, and all that. Too many ghosts in my past. My first team—you know what they did. And then you . . . you and me."

I rolled up my shirtsleeves. Suddenly, I hated the fact that I didn't wear a

T-shirt. I was burning the fuck up.

"No one knew about you and me. That's why I left, so you could have a clean break, a second chance. What the hell happened? Don't tell me you wasted everything I did for this fucking shit. Fuck."

I cursed for no reason and for every damn reason in front of me. The concept of Jules as a waitress wrecked me, thinking of random cocksuckers leering at her in that tie and tight oxford shirt while she worked for tips, forced to endure sleazy come-ons.

"I gave it all up for you. Thank fuck I did, but not for this second-class bullshit." Rage boiled up my spine, forcing me to spew angry words I knew I'd regret.

She moved away from the wall and started packing up her tote. Loosening her tie, she tugged it off and shoved it in the bag. She unbuttoned the top button of her shirt, and I saw hives spreading on her neck.

I couldn't stay put any longer; my body ached to get closer to her.

"Jules, what happened?" I traced the side of her neck with my finger, and she flinched. I didn't shy away, though. I couldn't even if I wanted. She was honey, and I was a bee.

Crap, I'm a goner. Done for this woman.

"Where's your *J*?"

"Don't. It's gone with Jules. Please don't touch me."

"I never meant to hurt you. I left for you. Believe me when I say the last few years have been hard for me, thinking about you, wondering what you're doing. Thoughts of you have consumed me on too many nights to count."

She closed her eyes and shook her head. "Please . . ."

I didn't care what she wanted; I was going to have my say. I'd waited long enough.

I took her hand and laced her fingers with mine, wondering why her calluses from playing were gone. I knew each and every one of them, just like I'd memorized the freckles dotting her skin.

"I was falling for you, in every way imaginable. I couldn't coach you when all I wanted to do was love you, protect you, ravage you. My feelings were on my sleeve. There was no way no one would notice."

She tugged her hand from mine. "It's fine, Drew. We overstepped boundaries, but that was a long time ago. I'm guessing you live near here, so if you can't keep your distance, I'll be forced to move."

"What?" Her reaction sent me reeling, mystified and unable to comprehend what she was saying. "You didn't care for me at all? You're leaving? For where?"

"It's a nonissue now. Life has moved on."

"But here we are, standing in front of each other." No way I was letting her slip through my grasp. Not again.

"It's been seven years. It's long over. If you'll excuse me, I have to go. It's been great seeing you. Seeing you're good, healthy, and well. Makes me feel good." She waved her hand up and down my body.

I watched her swallow a lump in her throat. Was it a lump of regret? Or need?

As she brushed by me, I realized there was something missing from her eyes. A small light had been extinguished, and I wanted to light it again. But she was rushing past me and nearly out the back door before I could grab her and keep her.

Keep her?

Maybe that was it. Maybe there was someone else.

"Wait! Jules . . . Claire . . . let me walk you to your car." I had to know what my competition was. Whoever it was, I planned to take them down fast.

She waved me off and slipped out the door, the heavy metal banging on its frame just as I got there. I swung it open, hearing it bang again behind my back as I made my way toward her. She beeped the locks on a smart-looking sedan and opened the back door on the driver's side.

"Please, wait," I said, breathless, more from nerves than a lack of stamina. I reached for her arm, the one stuffing her tote in the backseat.

"Don't!" she yelled, louder than I thought necessary.

"Am I hurting you?" Immediately, remorse coursed through my veins. What did I do? I'd never been forceful or rough when it wasn't welcome.

"Just don't, King. Don't." She shrugged the bag off her wrist and onto the floorboard, slamming the door when she was done. "Please, let me go."

Her words rang in my ears, but I couldn't take my eyes off my reflection. There I was in the window, the floodlight illuminating my sharp features, my short hair, the bump in my nose where it had been broken decades ago, and on the other side of the glass was . . . a child's car seat?

I blinked, certain my mind was playing tricks on me. Surely, she wasn't married? I hadn't seen a ring, and I was pretty sure I looked. Besides, what kind of schmuck would let someone as beautiful as Jules wait tables for a living on a Saturday night? She should be on an evening out, on a date with me.

"Leave it," she said.

My hand pressed against the glass. "No. I won't leave it. What the hell is going on with you waitressing? What, do you nanny during the day?" It was the only plausible explanation I could come up with.

"Something like that," she said, not meeting my eyes.

I tipped her chin toward me. "What about your degree?"

"I didn't stay at school after you left."

"What? That's why I left."

A tear formed in the corner of her left eye. When it fell in slow motion onto her cheek and slid toward her lip, I reached out and swiped it off with my thumb.

"Please tell me why you would do that. I've always dreamed you became successful, went on to do something amazing. I looked for you everywhere. Google, the news, Facebook, always praying you made good on your life. Why are you crying?"

"I had to leave," she said in a hushed voice. "I couldn't play anymore."

"Because of me?" I wrapped my arms around her and held her close, then kissed the top of her head. "Please say it wasn't because of me."

"I had a baby," she whispered.

"A baby?" Rocked to my very core, I shook my head, unable to believe what I'd just heard. "When?"

CHAPTER 15

Jules

One brush of his lips on my forehead, and I caved. Gave in, offered everything up. Every last ounce of protection burst from my body and my hardened shell cracked, allowing my mouth to utter the word I hadn't meant to share.

Baby.

It's why I left. I knew if I didn't run away, I'd confess it all. Drew was too powerful a force, and deep down in my heart, I knew if I'd told him, he'd have done right by me. But if he had, I never would have known if it was for me, or for the child.

His breath, his lips, his words all ghosting over me, rippling over my skin and setting my heart afire—it was all too much, a rush like no other.

"I had a baby."

Silence blanketed the parking lot, the only noise our combined erratic heartbeats. Together, our hearts were like a salsa band playing in a street festival.

"A baby? When?"

I told myself to lie, to make something up, but the truth bubbled in my gut. I tried to tamp it down, but I wasn't going to win this battle.

It was as if God was punishing me for telling Darla the truth. I should have told her a lie, that she didn't have a dad or some other bullshit. Then she wouldn't have wished to see him so badly.

It's like she'd conjured him up—the man who'd knocked me up was standing in front of me, asking about my baby. He seemed to have magically appeared out of thin air.

"I have a little girl. She just turned six in July."

I figured he could do the math, and make what he wanted out of the date.

He still stood silent, his arm firm around my back, his eyes never moving from mine. When his brow furrowed, I was finally able to confirm that the crinkles around his eyes had in fact deepened.

"I'm good with numbers. You remember that, right? So, was there someone else? Someone after me? Who the fuck got you pregnant?" His voice was angry and hurt, his pupils inky depths amidst the storm brewing in his eyes. "Did this guy hurt you? Ace, I mean Coach Hall, never mentioned anything. He never said you had a baby."

I looked at the ground, the black asphalt more consoling than sea blue. "There wasn't anyone else after you or during you."

He broke free and leaned his forearms on the car. Thank God, his long sleeves had fallen back down. After a moment, he lifted his head and looked at me dead-on.

"So the baby, the little girl . . . What the hell, Claire?" My new name came out on a snarl. "She's mine? Ours?"

My gaze dropped to the asphalt.

"Is this a fucking dream? A nightmare? Who the hell are you? And how dare you say this shit now?" He continued to rant, his jaw clenched, angrier than I'd ever seen him.

His large frame pulled away from the car and loomed over me, his hands on my shoulders, forcing me to look up. "And why exactly did you decide to keep this from me?"

"You left." My words were a soft gurgle, a pathetic mewling.

"You've heard of Google? Right, Claire? I know you didn't have a smartphone back then, but surely you've outgrown all that bullshit. Especially

71

now that you're a *mom*." He spat out the last word with a snarl on his face.

"Just like you left, wanting a better life for me, I didn't want any repercussions for you."

"Coach Hall knew how to reach me too."

"I wasn't sure it mattered to you. That she mattered to you. Darla—"

I caught myself, unsure what had compelled me to use her name. It didn't feel right, tossing her back and forth in verbal jabs like an inanimate object. She was a person named Darla.

"I don't believe you. This is fucking absurd. It's bullshit. We didn't make a baby." And just like that, he stormed off.

As for me, I got into my car and drove home. Once I'd paid the sitter, I crawled into my bed, where Darla had snuck in to sleep.

Pulling her to my chest and inhaling the scent of her hair, breathing in the sweet strawberry smell that lingered from her bath, I decided it was for the best. Drew didn't think she was his, and therefore, he was done with me.

It made my decision to stay far away from him easier.

CHAPTER 16

Drew

I ditched the rest of the dinner, went home, stripped off my clothes, and sat on the floor of my walk-in shower until the water ran cold. With my back pressed against the custom tile, my mind ran laps.

Am I really the father of a little girl named Darla?

What's her middle name?

Christ, when was her birthday?

When my body was shivering and pruned, I got out and crawled between the covers, soaking wet and naked. All night, I tossed and turned, beating down the urge to vomit.

A baby?

Does she like French fries? TV? Going to the playground?

Can she swim?

Does she know about me?

These questions and more plagued me into the early hours of the morning. Even my weariness couldn't overcome the depths of pain I felt. Finally, I rolled out of bed at dawn and went to the gym an hour earlier than usual for a Sunday.

"I'm watching the TV," I said curtly to the girl next to me, not caring how obnoxious I sounded.

I was in no mood to chat or date or be nice. In the course of twelve hours, the freedoms I'd known for the last few years were gone. My heart leaped at the opportunity to surrender itself to a little girl I'd never met, and the woman I'd always longed for.

I beat the hell out of the treadmill, running faster than my knee was comfortable with but fast enough to make my brain shut the fuck down. I couldn't even tell you what was on the television, but it was better than the two-bit coed making eyes at me, or the memory of the night before.

Visions of Jules flashed in my mind like that old-fashioned toy, a viewfinder. Sweat rolled from my forehead and down my face, stinging my eyes, and I blinked the visions away.

After abusing my knee on the treadmill, I showered, changed into my whites, grabbed a smoothie, and drove to the public tennis courts.

I didn't have it in me to ditch my commitments because my world had been shattered the night before. Once a month, the pros from my club ran a free tennis clinic in the park for kids and teens. I'd been involved for the last four years, and found it to be the most rewarding thing I'd ever done. Better than earning a few million in the market, or giving backspin tips to the privileged kids at the club.

The teens I worked with at the park didn't have all the advantages I'd been provided, and some of them showed real promise. They were hungry and wanted to win. Yes, I missed playing and coaching, and teaching only sated part of the hunger in me, but it was better than nothing.

"Hey, Drew," the head pro called to me. "Good to see you."

"Thanks, Derrick. You know I love this."

"I know. Way more than my young pros do, the pricks. Which is why I have to ask you a favor."

"Shoot." I shook my racquet out of the bag and tossed the grip between my hands.

"I know you love the teens, but we have a second session of the kinder clinic starting today. Susie usually teaches them, but she went to a wedding this weekend. And, well, you're the only one with enough patience to do it.

Most of them are returning kids."

"No problem. Which court?"

"The one over in the shade."

I didn't tell Derrick, but I welcomed the reprieve. Little kids were easy—a constant stream of light forehands and backhands, and they were happy. We could even do some volleys.

Two little boys waited for me, caps secured on their heads and shoes double-laced on their feet.

"Hey, boys, I'm Coach Drew. Who are you?"

"Stephen."

"Patrick. Where's Susie? She taught us last session."

"She had a commitment today, but she'll be back. Like I said, I'm Drew, and it's nice to meet you. Why don't we stretch a little on the baseline while we wait for a few others?"

I checked their secondhand racquets and grips, then ran them through a few stretches. Soon we were joined by Polly, Samantha, and Chris.

We were lining up on the baseline when I heard a child say, "Mom, I'm fine. I know how to hit. It's easy."

"Dar, let me just meet your instructor," said a familiar voice. "We're new here."

I turned and looked down at my freaking spitting image, who had long strawberry-blond hair. The little girl stared up at me with wide blue eyes, as familiar to me as my own, and I swallowed the lump in my throat.

"Hi, um, I'm Coach Drew. We were going to start with hitting forehands." I forced myself to speak through the angry recognition and sharp pain searing through my spine.

"I'm Darla. I'm new here, but I know what that is, a forehand. My mom was a tennis player, and so am I."

So was your dad.

The tiny spitfire marched right over to the baseline and took her place in line, spinning her grip and tossing the racquet from hand to hand.

I eyed the redheaded woman now standing off to the side, and tried not to shoot daggers her way. This was the woman I'd been so desperately in love with, I'd set aside all my own wants and needs for her happiness.

And what did she do?

She hid my kid.

"Drew," the sexy-as-hell witch whispered.

"Not now, not here." My tone was rougher than I wanted, but I was good and pissed. "Maybe not ever," I added, and for the briefest of moments, I believed it.

Without another word, she withdrew, stepping into the background, and I took my place on the opposite side of the net with my basket of balls.

"Did you all meet Darla?" My voice carried over to the line of children waiting for instruction.

A wave of *yeps* drifted across the net.

"Okay, we're going to each hit two forehands going across the baseline. Did Susie show you the right way to grip the racquet? Why don't you all show me?" I pointed to the two places I would hit the balls, and then looked over the net at their little hands gripping the racquets.

"One sec."

I crossed over to them and fixed Polly and Stephen's grips, adjusting their palms and fingers. And poor Samantha was so little, she could barely hold the weight of the racquet. I moved her hands up the grip and gave her a pat on her head.

Then there was Darla, her hands in perfect position over her bubblegum-pink grip. It was an expensive racquet, and I wondered how many tables her mom had to wait on to afford it.

"Looks good, Darla."

"My mom showed me. She was teaching me before we came here. Every day, all summer."

"Looks like she did a good job." I turned my back before she could see the pathetic display of emotion across my face.

I had a kid. A daughter who played tennis and wore her strawberry-blond hair down. *Unlike her mom.* A daughter I knew nothing more about.

Was she in school? Did she like dolls? What was her middle name?

What's her last name?

"Let's go, Coach Drew."

When Patrick jogged me out of my thoughts, I started serving up balls, and the kids made their way down the line. A miss, ball into the net, another miss, one over the net, miss, net, shot made. Then two perfect shots by Darla, just like her mom used to do.

The hour pretty much went the same. More forehands and a few backhands, the other kids making some and missing most, but Darla made every shot.

At the end of the session, I found some stickers tucked in the basket. I promised the kids that once they'd finished delivering a racquet face full of the scattered balls back into the bin, I'd give them each a sticker.

Darla was the third to finish picking up balls. Her hair was wind-blown all around her face, and her cheeks were golden instead of red like the others.

"Thanks," she said as I handed her a sticker.

"You're going to be some player," I said quietly, not wanting to upset the others.

"My mom said one day I'd go to college and play tennis and then be a doctor, but I want to be a real tennis player on TV. We watch them sometimes."

The other kids filed past for their stickers. Each one thanked me and ran off to their parents sitting by the gazebo.

Except for Darla. She was still chattering about the tennis players on TV.

"Come on, Dar. Let Coach Drew go," her mom called from the side of the court.

"Okay. 'Bye, Coach Drew," she called as she ran to Jules.

I memorized her purple shorts and pink T-shirt, the shape of her small legs as she ran, and the way she beamed at her mom. Jules kissed her on the top of her head, and they made their way to the park exit.

"Wait!" I called out as I ran up the hill after them, my knee not happy with me after the punishment it took on the treadmill this morning.

When I caught up, I focused on the child. "Darla, on the other Sundays of the month, I teach at Rocky Brook's tennis club. You could come to my class. What grade are you in?"

"First. With Ms. Green. She's super nice."

"You know what? You're good enough to play with the older kids. Or I could give you private lessons."

She jumped up and down, her hair a swirling mess around her face.

"Then I'll be on TV, Mom!"

Jules frowned at me. "I'm not sure that's in our budget, Drew. Let me talk with Darla at home."

"At no cost, on me," I said, not about to be denied. I was a thirsty man in the desert.

"No, no. I don't do things like that."

"But, Mom! I'm bored playing with you."

"Don't do this. I don't want your pity," Jules said through gritted teeth.

"But I want to. She's—" I got a death stare at that. Clearly, I wasn't to mention that Darla was my daughter. But who the hell did she think was her father? "I was going to say she's very talented."

"She is. It's in her blood."

"It most definitely is."

"Mom, I'm thirsty. I'm going over to the fountain."

When Darla was out of earshot, I gave Jules a hard look. "You can't keep her from me."

"You just said an hour ago that you didn't ever want to talk about this."

"I didn't. Now I do. Forgive me for the whiplash, but it's probably warranted. I just found out, and I don't even know if she has a middle name or my last name."

"You left."

Jules's hair was in that stupid put-together bun she wore now. I wanted to rip it the fuck out and kiss her silly. Or punch her in the gut. I'd never hit a woman before, and I didn't plan on doing it. But still.

"Darla Katherine Smith. Katherine with a K."

"So you gave my child my initials but never intended to allow her to meet me? To know me?" When Jules pressed her lips together but didn't respond, I pushed harder. "I want to see my daughter, and since she has no clue who I am, this is how I'm going to do it."

Darla came running back over to us. "Let's go, Mom! You said we were going to paint our nails too."

She jumped around on one pink tennis shoe with her other leg in the air. Then she switched hopping feet, doing a little jig on the concrete. For a minute, I thought she had to pee, but she didn't look uncomfortable. In fact, she was singing to herself, and she was so freaking adorable, I hated to interrupt.

"See you next Sunday, Darla. Your mom said yes; you can come take lessons with me."

"Woo-hoo!" She threw her arms around her mom's waist, hugging her.

"Just come on by Rocky Brook around ten. Sound good?"

When Jules did nothing more than nod, the score wasn't love–fifteen anymore. It was fifteen–all, and I was going to get a chance to spend time with my daughter.

I'd say the advantage was all mine, even if that wasn't the right way to keep score.

79

CHAPTER 17

Drew

The week dragged on. Unable to calm my mind, I was opening and closing the gym each day, trying to calm my body. I'd canceled lunch with Sully, and sent younger associates to all of my other lunch meetings.

Besides sweating at the gym and moping at my office, I spent several nights staring out my floor-to-ceiling windows, looking for nothing and hoping for everything. I showered but didn't shave.

By Thursday, my whole face itched from the scruff, and my entire body shook with fury. I wasn't going to make it to Sunday, so I let go of my impulse control and drove right to the Southern Steak and Sea.

I couldn't remember where we had our portfolio meetings before the Southern opened, and it had only been a month. It seemed like my entire existence broke off and fell into the ocean a few nights ago, right here at the Southern.

I pulled up to the valet and hopped out, smoothing my untucked oxford and making sure my Pumas were tied.

A young brunette wearing a black slinky dress and red stilettos greeted me inside. "Welcome to the Southern."

I ran my hand over my scruff and tried to scan the room behind her.

"Two?" she guessed.

"Actually, one."

"Did you want to eat in our bar area? We serve a full menu in there." She stepped out from behind the hostess stand, willing me to eye her up.

"No, thank you. I'd like a table for one. In Claire's section."

"Oh." Her face fell and she went back to her iPad. "I don't think we have anything in Claire's section. It's full right now, and we have a window-table reservation coming in shortly."

I dug into my pocket and pulled out a crisp Ben Franklin. When I laid it on the hostess stand and gave it a tap, her gaze lifted again to size me up.

"Let me see. Maybe I can move the reservation."

"You do that."

My patience was wearing thin. The place was busy, but not jam-packed enough that Jules wouldn't spot me. I wanted to sneak into her section. Lord knew, she'd protest or run out of here.

I kept my gaze on the floor, dreaming of Jules and her legs. Her long legs were now a little curvier, more muscular.

"Right this way."

I avoided making eye contact with the rest of the room as the brunette led me to my table in a quiet corner next to the window. Clearly, the window-reservation people were going to be unhappy.

Oh well. Fuck 'em.

"Thanks." I dismissed the hostess, sat, grabbed my menu and hid behind it, pretending to study the offerings as if there was going to be a test later.

"Welcome to the Southern. I'm Claire."

I dropped the menu slowly, revealing my face. It was an old trick straight out of an eighties movie, but a useful one.

"Drew," she said my name on a breath, then practically hissed, "Come on, I'm working." She glanced around the room as if worried we had an audience.

"I had to see you, Jules," I said, whispering her real name.

"I can't do this. I need this job."

"I know. I'll wait. Look at me—I haven't slept all week, and I need to talk with you."

81

"I'm not done until eleven tonight."

"I can wait right here. Why don't you bring me a Scotch and soda?"

She stepped a little closer and pretended to take notes on a notepad as she said, "I have to go home after my shift. I'm not some young coed who can fall into bed with you. I have Darla."

"Shit, you think I just want to fuck you?" I slammed my fist onto the table, furious with myself for forgetting child care and shit.

"You didn't think about that, did you? About her?"

I'd forgotten how well Jules could read me. "Where is Darla? Who's with her? This parenting thing is all new to me."

"She's with a sitter. Because I'm working."

"Well, I can come home with you . . . later."

"I don't think so, Drew."

She pursed her lips, and her dumb fucking tight-ass bun taunted me. I wanted to grab the purple tie she wore around her neck and yank her close, kiss that pissy look right off her face, bury my tongue in her mouth and sink my free hand in her hair.

"To talk," I lied.

"I'm not ready. I agreed to the tennis lessons, but that's it. Look, I have to go. I have other tables."

"I still want my Scotch, and I'm going to order some food."

She turned without saying a word.

A few minutes later, some asshole arrived with my drink and asked if I needed anything else.

"Of course," I told him. "But I'll wait for Claire to put my order in."

That was pretty much how the evening went. I barked drink orders at Jules, and she sent other people to deliver them. She dumped my steak in front of me, and it wasn't clear whether she'd been aiming for my lap.

The back-and-forth left me pretty much wrecked and sauced by the time her shift ended.

"I'm finishing up for the evening, so if you want to close out your bill . . ." She stood beside my table, her arms crossed, surveying me with a dirty look. "Or I can transfer it over to someone else."

I whipped out my black card and handed it to her. "I'll close out."

When she returned with my bill, she said quietly, "I'm going to call you a cab. You're drunk, and I don't want that responsibility on my hands."

"You drive me. Please, Jules." I stood and misjudged, rattling the table, sending the leftover ice sloshing in my tumbler.

"Drew."

When she came close, I could smell her perfume. It reminded me of sea and beach and sand. It was new on her, but I liked it anyway.

"My sitter is waiting."

"Tell her to wait. I'll pay." I reached into my pocket and pulled out my money clip.

"No. Why would you do that?"

"She's my daughter, Jules, that's why. And you're waiting tables in a steak joint to make ends meet. That's further why," I said, and leaned my head onto her shoulder.

"Don't."

Sadly, I listened like a scolded puppy and moved.

"One second." She walked to the side of the restaurant and pulled out her phone.

I watched her fingers graze the little screen, typing quickly, and imagined she was running them over my chest and into my pants . . .

Shit. I ran my hand over my face and got my head straight. I was hoping to talk. Not touch.

Maybe just a little?

When the screen in her hand illuminated with a reply, she said, "Come on," to me and pointed toward the back exit.

I waited for her while she gathered her stuff, and we walked out into the night air. It was muggy and humid enough, but when I saw Jules finally let down her hair, I found it hard to breathe. She yanked on the hair tie and all her red glory fell around her face. I searched for her green eyes in the lion's mane in front of me.

My hand twitched to move up and push her hair out of the way . . . guiding my lips to hers.

"Drew! Drew, stop."

Looks like my hand more than twitched.

"I'm sorry." I breathed into her hair, unable to take my fingers out of it. Placing my lips on her forehead, I bared my soul. "I'm so confused, Jules. I spent the last seven years trying to put you in some sort of storage bin in my brain. I worked, worked out, ate, and drank, but I didn't live."

Her hand came to rest on my elbow, her fingers lightly grazing my skin.

"Now, here you are. Alive and well, looking amazing . . . and you had my daughter. And all of that is messing with my head. I want you. Need you. I never stopped loving you."

She squeezed my elbow. "We can't. I can't. Our past is our past and it has to stay there, Drew. I'm not going to keep Darla from you, but that's all that you get out of this deal. Darla. On my terms."

"Please." The word was mangled, coming from somewhere deep in my gut.

"Come on, I'm going to drive you home. Besides being drunk, you're talking nonsense."

She moved away, opened the driver's side door and got in her sedan, and I slithered into the passenger's side like the snake I was.

I might have been drunk, but a thousand and one scenarios ran through my mind . . . how to get Jules in my bed and my daughter under my roof.

What the fuck? What the hell happened to me?

The big dick-swinging bachelor, the hard-ass coach who fell into lust with his collegiate player?

He fell in love and never forgot it.

CHAPTER 18

Jules

My car idled outside his place, not your typical Floridian Spanish stucco monstrosity, or one of those big mega-mansions with the hideous Roman columns.

No, it was worse.

Much, much worse.

Perfectly worse.

Modern white clapboard siding lit by the moonlight outlined the two-story house situated on the coastal highway. I rolled down the window and listened to the ocean slap against the shore as I took in the modern take on a Craftsman in front of me. It was like the 1970s *Brady Bunch* house impregnated one of those ridiculous industrial-modern places, and they created the most stunning place known to man.

Drew swayed a bit as he made his way down a narrow walkway and up a few steps toward the front door. I couldn't help but silently pray he fell into his perfectly trimmed bushes.

The air smelled like salt and money. I took in the private staircase down to the beach as the light popped on inside Drew's house. It was a dream and a nightmare. This could have been mine . . . but it wasn't.

Needing to get back to where I belonged, I started to reverse out of the driveway, needing to leave this fantasy in my rearview.

"Jules," he called out, and I stopped until he caught up to me. "I meant it. I've always loved you. Please give me a chance."

"Good night, Drew."

It was time to return to reality, I scolded myself, to my small two-bedroom apartment, far away from the water. I needed to stay in my lane and away from Drew.

After dropping Darla off at school the next day, I sat slumped over my morning coffee, visions of his gorgeous house tormenting me. It was a fantasy.

Drew was then and this is now. Me, Darla, the apartment situated in a decent school district, and the promise of Bryce moving on and me taking over his job.

The Southern chain had been good to me ever since Bryce had taken a chance on me. I'd been given stacked benefits and the opportunity to build a life for my daughter and me. As the company expanded, they promoted from within, and seniority counted. Perhaps soon, I'd be a manager.

My mom had wanted me to give up the baby and finish my degree, but I couldn't do it. The tiny life in my belly had become my entire purpose as soon as I learned about it—about her.

There was no way I could have stayed in Ohio, and my mom wouldn't leave. My dad had been buried there when I was two. She'd die there too, and be buried next to him and the countless memories she had, no doubt half of them make-believe.

Plus, she'd made it clear she wasn't going to help with the baby.

Even when she'd shown up in North Carolina for the delivery, she'd said every ten minutes, "I'm going home in a few days, and you're on your own."

When I'd fled to North Carolina at the promise of a tennis-teaching gig and a whisper of night school, it had been a pipe dream. Neither panned out for a twenty-something single mom.

Over the years, my mom had looked at Darla with suspicion. On Dar's third Christmas, Mom came to visit again, bringing a few presents and a pocketful of accusations.

Actually, her accusations were truths. *"I'd know that face, those eyes anywhere."*

My phone rang, interrupting my negative-thought train.

When I saw who it was, I answered, "I'm not working lunch, Bryce. I promised Darla I'd pick her up at school and see the turtle in their classroom."

"Nice. But I'm not calling about lunch."

"Oh, sorry." I went to the coffeemaker and topped off my mug. "What's up?"

Bryce cleared his throat, something he did when he was nervous.

"What?" I demanded.

"Your friend is here. He came to pick up his car, and he asked for your phone number."

"Ugh." I slumped back into my seat.

"He's refusing to leave until I give it to him."

"I'll come and deal with him."

"You sure? You don't have to—I can handle him."

"See you soon."

I hung up and yanked out my messy bun. With a swift hand, I finger-combed through the knots and twisted my hair into a tight knot. I threw a cardigan over the tank and yoga pants I'd worn to school drop-off, and slipped my feet into flip-flops.

It didn't take me long to make my way to the restaurant. As I pulled around back, I caught Drew sitting next to the back door. He was in athletic shorts and a damp shirt, his feet straight out from him, adorned in running shoes.

I slammed the car in park and jumped out. "Drew!"

I was good and mad, but for all the wrong reasons. Furious at the man in front of me for reigniting a dream that had died long ago. Devastated that I refused to allow myself to have the fantasy, the reunion I'd seen in my mind about a million times.

When he stood and headed slowly toward me, all the anger seeped from my veins.

"Why are you limping?"

"It's fine. I'm fine."

"Are you hurt? Don't tell me you ran here—"

"I ran at the gym. Ubered there, Ubered here. Would've Ubered to you . . . if I knew where that was."

"You can't keep surprising me like this."

"I can and I will. Until you give me what I want."

He closed the gap between us; close enough for me to see the beads of sweat that clung to his short hair, and detect his scent. He smelled like sweat and something minty.

"I want you," he said on a breath. "And I'm going to have you."

I couldn't speak; my lungs didn't work. I commanded myself to take in air and blow it out my nose. "Drew," I said, as if his name were the only word in my vocabulary.

"Have you eaten?"

I shook my head to clear the cobwebs of confusion—he was like an emotional boomerang this morning—but he took it as my response.

"Great. Let's go eat." He flung his arm around me and pulled me against his side, grazing my ear with his lips.

"I'm not dressed to eat . . . to go anywhere."

"Sure you are. You just need to do this." He tugged on my knot and gave my hair free rein to do what it wanted, which was to curl around my face.

"Drew."

"Enough with my name. I know who I am. And what happened to King Drew?"

"He left," I said bitterly.

"He didn't want to."

As if on cue, my stomach gurgled.

"Come on. I'm going to feed you."

With his arm wrapped around me, Drew guided me to a ritzy twenty-four-hour diner just a block away. I hadn't eaten at the Purple Stallion yet, mostly because it was out of my price range with all the expensive tennis equipment I had to buy, and the upcoming birthday party.

88

We walked inside the metal building, fashioned after an old-school diner, and a brass bell chimed overhead. The inside was all shades of purple, from the linoleum to a huge glass-shelved bar lining the back. TVs hung over the bar, and miniature carousel ponies dangled from the ceiling. The place was outrageously gaudy and super cool at the same time.

The smell of fresh-brewed coffee and cinnamon filled the air, making my stomach growl.

Drew flashed the hostess two fingers, never letting me go.

"Toward the back," he said in a hushed tone when the hostess came close. "Something semi-private, a booth?"

"Gotcha." She led us to a small booth in the back, a window on one side and the drink station on the other.

I slid into the booth, and rather than sit opposite me, Drew squeezed in next to me. His thigh hit mine, and I would like to say I wasn't a goner, but I was.

Heat, old feelings, unanswered questions, and new curiosities clung to every cell in my body.

CHAPTER 19

Jules

"Hey, welcome to the Stallion. Old-timers or virgins?"

I wondered if the waitress was some sort of clairvoyant. Drew and I were definitely old-timers when it came to each other, and definitely not virgins.

Of course, she barely glanced at me, yet couldn't keep her batty eyes off Drew.

"Two coffees, milk instead of cream," he said, ignoring her cute face, blatant flirting, and curvy physique. Instead, he turned to face me.

"I still take milk."

Crap, I don't why that came out of my mouth.

"I figured." His finger caught a loose hair, pushed it behind my ear, and he leaned close.

"I know. That was stupid of me. I'm all out of focus or brains when it comes to you. Just like old times, but I have no idea what it means." With him in my personal space, my voice was quiet and timid, my brain barely able to fire synapses.

"Don't do that." He kissed my cheek. "Don't be hesitant with me, because all I want is you."

Right then, little Miss Peppy Server set the coffees on the table, my milk in a small container on the side.

"Did you know what you want?" she said, still focusing on Drew.

"We didn't even look yet. What do you recommend?"

"The special is crepes. They're filled with Chantilly crème and topped with fresh raspberries. It's divine." This declaration brought her tongue out, and she licked her lips, making me wonder if this was a porno or a diner. "Today's sausage is organic apple-spiced chicken. My personal favorite is the sweet potato pancakes with cranberry-apple compote."

"Great. Bring us the special and potato pancakes to start."

"Be back," she said, and left us.

"I could've ordered for myself."

"I know, but I wanted her gone."

I poured some milk into my mug and took a sip of the coffee, the liquid warming my throat and lifting my mood.

"I'm going to win you back."

Drew reached out and his hand covered mine. I watched the veins flex and the hair on his forearm like they were Beyoncé in the halftime show during the Super Bowl. I didn't want to take my eyes away for a second.

"Who said I'm a prize to win?" I spoke without lifting my gaze, and of course, he tilted my chin up with his finger.

"You're not just the prize. You're everything, and I want it. I want you and my daughter. All of us, together."

"I can't."

"Don't say that. You can, and you will."

As he ran his lips along my cheek, a faint reminder of how much he drank the night before wafted from his pores and mixed with the mint.

"God, I want you so bad," he mumbled.

"It's not like that now. I have a daughter." My standard line seemed wrong in this moment; not that I'd used it a lot.

"*We* have a daughter."

I sealed my eyes shut and allowed every thought, every concern about Darla to wash over me. "I'm such an idiot. How will I tell her who you are?

I've fucked this up beyond repair."

"Nothing is beyond repair, especially us."

He squeezed my hand, and I wanted to believe him.

"Here you go."

The server was back with two plates. The air around us filled with sweet aromas, reminding me I was famished.

Drew stopped the server as she was walking away. "Oh, can I get an order of the sausage for myself?" Turning to me, he said, "I didn't want it to touch your crepe. The meat."

Why did he have to be so thoughtful?

"Not necessary, but thanks." I picked up my fork and took a bite of crepe and raspberry, moaning as the crème made its way around my mouth.

"Wish you were doing that for me."

Raising an eyebrow at him, I said, "You're really into the cheesy now."

"Nah." He ran his finger down my forearm. "Just trying to lighten the mood for my girl."

"Drew," I growled.

"My soon-to-be girl."

"Don't you have work?" I asked around a mouthful of cranberry and potato.

"I haven't got much done this week. Plus the hangover. I left my associates in charge."

"Finance?"

"Yeah, risky investments with high returns. It's all about the thrill for my people."

"Wow. I don't know if I could gamble with my money like that."

"Most of my clients have plenty to spare. As for me, I didn't think I had much responsibility until a few days ago. Now I have a love child . . ."

I couldn't help myself. I laughed out loud. "Love child! You make it sound so sinister."

"But it is, isn't it? Our story? A coach and his pupil make a child."

"Oh God, just eat and soak up the alcohol. *Pupil.*" I rolled my eyes and almost laughed the coffee right out of my nose at that word.

"Oh, I sweat that shit out already. My knee wasn't happy, but my gut was."

92

He speared a crepe just as his sausage arrived. "Now, tell me about Darla Katherine King."

"Smith," I corrected him.

"Hopefully not for long, but I'll let it be. Tell me, how big was she when she was born? Did she come out with a racquet in her tiny hand? What's her damn birthday?"

I breathed a sigh of relief for the first time in forever. It dawned on me, I'd never really shared these memories aloud. "She weighed seven pounds, four ounces at birth. Came out screaming like a banshee on July twentieth, demanding to eat. Took to my breast right away . . ."

A moan escaped Drew's mouth.

"What? That's how babies eat, King."

"I'm not grossed out. It's just the thought of your nipple, hard and wet. It does something to me. And you should be thankful because I was a venomous asshole when I fell asleep last night. Somehow the thoughts of you caring for Darla have calmed my rage."

"Drink your coffee and be quiet. It's food. Sustenance. Not a sexual endeavor. As for your temper, control it. You're the one who left. Not me."

"Wait . . . is she a vegetarian?"

"Nice way to change the topic. Yep, she is." I wrapped my hands around my warm mug, a smug look on my face.

"You're gonna ruin her. Is she growing enough? On all those beans and sprouts?"

"She's growing just fine."

"So, you take her to the doctor and dentist and all that. Does she need braces? What about glasses? Her shots—does she have all of them?"

"Whoa, now. I'm her mom. She goes everywhere she needs to go, eats everything she needs to eat, takes her vitamins. She still has her baby teeth, for Christ's sake."

Drew semi-laughed while giving me a dirty look, and continued with his barrage of questions.

We drank coffee and talked over breakfast as if we'd never missed seven years.

CHAPTER 20

Drew

"So Darla's at school?" I'd been asking nonstop questions since our food came. Jules had been mostly patient with me, except when I'd mentioned Darla's last name.

She nodded as we walked back toward the Southern and her car.

"I still want to know more about her. What was she like as a baby? Demanding like now? Did you have help? Your mom?"

Jules shook her head. "Gah, this is all too much. Do we have to do this now? We've wasted almost the whole day with your information gathering. And I don't even have your phone number."

I wrapped my arm around her and pulled her close. "We have time on our side now, but I want to know every detail. In the meantime, give me your phone." When she handed it to me, I punched in my number and called myself. "There."

She pulled away from me and stopped. "We don't have much time. Not now, not really any time. I work, and I have Darla. That's been the story of my life for six years. I want more for her. College, a life. Speaking of which, I have to grab her from school soon and then work tonight. Bryce is letting me come in a little late because Dar's teacher is letting her show me the class turtle today."

"Great. Let's go." I put my hand on her back and encouraged her to move.

"I've been doing this a long time on my own, Drew. Six years, remember? My mom couldn't commit to help either way, but it didn't matter. I needed to leave Ohio and the memory of you."

"It's just a turtle." I took her into my arms, circling her in a hug in broad daylight for everyone to see. *She's mine.*

It was an invigorating feeling. Liberating. Something I hadn't been able to do seven years ago.

"How do you propose we explain your being there?"

"Who cares?"

"Me. Darla. Her teacher."

"We don't owe anyone any explanations today, Jules. Darla, yes, someday soon. But let me just go meet the fucking turtle, okay?"

She nodded into my chest, and I silently pleaded for her to place a kiss there. She didn't.

"You need to follow me there. I need to bring Dar home in my own car, though. I'm not changing my mind on that."

"Okay, my queen."

"Will you please stop with the cheese?" She punched my arm, but couldn't hide the smile spreading across her face.

"You want cheese?"

I pushed her into her sedan and followed her, looming over her. My pelvis pressed against her stomach, my hardness making delicious contact with her softness.

I ran my tongue up her neck. "I'll give you cheese anytime you want it. Just say the word and I can be as corny and cocky as you want."

I'd said it laughing and gyrating, and even though it was a cornball move, Jules laughed too, her light giggle filling the air around us. Seeing her smile, I gave my pelvis another rotation.

"Okay, enough, enough, corny and cocky."

I let her go and kissed the bridge of her nose. "As you wish, my queen."

"Oh God."

"No, king . . ."

"Drew, come on. We have to go. Do you know the elementary school?"

I shook my head. How the hell would I know the elementary school?

"Follow me, okay?"

"Forever and ever."

This got me an eye roll.

And a smile.

"Mom!" Darla bolted down the steps in front of her school. "Come on!"

The bell had rung and kids were running around everywhere, looking for buses and parents.

"Coach Drew, what are you doing here?"

Darla pivoted in her hot-pink sneakers, her hand on her hip, questioning me as if she was Oprah. I couldn't help it; I fell deeper and deeper for her incredible sense of confidence and running commentary.

I was standing across from Jules with Darla in the middle as I watched Jules's eyes cloud with hesitation. Her daughter might have been full of confidence, but Jules wasn't.

I made the decision to ad-lib. "You know what?"

"What?" Darla turned to me, big blue eyes wide and her hair a wild mess.

"Your mom and I knew each other back when she played tennis. We both figured it out the other day after the lesson. You're new to town, and lucky for you, I'm not . . . so I get to show you around."

"Really?" Her smile spread wide and she started jumping up and down. "But you're still going to teach me tennis?"

"Yep. But first, I'm going to meet this turtle."

"Why don't you lead the way, Dar?" Jules took our daughter's hand but not mine.

That's okay. Baby steps. I was here, so it didn't matter who held her hand.

We walked back into the building, and Jules turned and mouthed *thank you* as we went through the door.

"Hello there. I'm Ms. Green," a short brunette said when we entered

Darla's classroom. "You must be Claire. And you are . . ." Her gaze pinged between Darla and me, circling back and forth a few times as she waited for an introduction.

"I'm a friend. Drew." I stuck out my hand and cut off Ms. Green before she said something Jules would regret.

"Well, let's show your mom and her friend our turtle, Raphael."

"Isn't that like the movie?"

"It is." Ms. Green laughed, sliding her glasses on top of her head and sticking her chest out. She was feeling a vibe I wasn't giving.

"Mom, Mom, Coach Drew, look!" A medium-sized turtle crawled around inside the tank, miniature shrubbery flanking the perimeter. "Isn't he cute?"

Jules chuckled and nodded. "He is." She swiped Darla's hair behind her neck and twisted it into a knot.

"Mom, leave it. Look at Raphael." Darla swatted behind her at Jules's hand. She was definitely my daughter. "I want one!"

"Dar, you know we discussed this."

"I know." Darla's tiny body slumped, but she still glowed while watching the damn turtle.

Looks like I'll be buying a pet. Wish she'd look at me like that.

Ms. Green leaned against the desk, the chalkboard behind her with a rainbow in the middle. "Darla has been a lovely addition to the class. I met most of the students at the end of last year, and they're a nice group. I knew there wouldn't be any problem introducing a new student."

"Thank you so much for saying that. It hasn't been too hard, the move . . . and she's young and resilient."

"That she is," Ms. Green said, looking at me.

Uncomfortable, I stared at the colorful carpet. Did Darla and I look that much alike?

I raised my eyes and looked at Darla's profile. Yep, she was a mirror image of me but with her mom's wild hair, its shade somewhere between Jules's and mine.

There was no way we could keep up this charade for much longer.

CHAPTER 21

Jules

As Darla and I pulled away from the school, she was one big tumbleweed of words. Raphael, what turtles eat, and when they poop. Drew's car was so cool. Ms. Green was so pretty.

Yes, she was, and I couldn't help but notice her making eyes at Drew. I wanted to say I wasn't jealous, but I was. Terribly.

At home, I made Darla an early dinner.

"Mom, I don't ever want to eat fish sticks. It's like eating a cousin of Rafe's. I'm a vegetarian like you."

"Darla, fish is actually good for you. It's protein, and you need that for your brain. You know, some people are pescatarians. That's the only source of animal protein they eat. Fish is so good for you," I said, and Drew's questions about Darla's diet came back to me.

What I hadn't told him was the new doctor did suggest some additional protein for Darla, especially since she was so into tennis and needed it for her growing muscles. But I wasn't about to reveal my shortcomings or failures to Drew or anyone else. I did the best I could.

"I'm eating the broccoli. That's healthy."

"Don't fool me; you're eating it because it tastes good. And that's because I drizzled butter on it."

"Mom, please? I don't want fish."

It was a lost cause. Darla was a stubborn as they came.

"You need something more than buttery broccoli. How about some beans and cheese?"

"Sure!"

Just as the microwave dinged, signaling the cheesy beans were ready, my doorbell rang. Darla popped out of her chair and ran to answer the door.

"Hi, Molly," she said, then dashed back to the table.

I gave Molly a wave. "Hey. I have to scat, but Darla is eating, and then she needs to do a half hour of reading practice before any TV. I know it's Friday, but we can have fun all weekend."

"No prob, Claire."

Molly sat down next to Darla, and immediately the two started chatting as I gathered my things to leave for work.

" . . . and you know, my mom has a friend named Drew from when she played tennis, and he came to see Raphael."

Shit.

Molly looked at me and raised an eyebrow. We'd only known each other a little more than a month, but she was the closest person to family I'd had in a long time.

I shook my head and waved my hand as if Drew were nothing, not my baby daddy or anything like that.

"I have to close tonight, so I'll be late. Thanks, Molly." I leaned over Darla's head, breathing in her little-girl scent as I kissed the top of her head. "Love you, baby girl. See you in the morning."

Luckily, the Southern was jammed when I arrived, and I didn't have a second to dwell on my day . . . until Drew sat down in my section close to nine.

He was freshly showered, smelling like tea-tree oil and sex appeal. He sat with his hands on the table, his oxford shirt rolled up to the elbows and the top buttons undone. I couldn't help but look more closely to see he was wearing jeans and a pair of scuffed Gucci loafers. It didn't matter how hard he tried; he couldn't shake the prep-boy image.

The lunacy of our situation grew with every second I stood by his table, waiting for him to say something.

"Do you want my usual *Welcome to the Southern* spiel?"

He shook his head as he eyed me, his blue eyes narrowed on mine. Without a word, he licked his lips and continued to drink me in.

"Then why aren't you saying anything?"

"I'm staring at you, taking in all that is Claire. To me, you're the same, but all new. I miss the messy bun and the short shorts, but I'm just as intrigued by the competent woman you've become. Though, I'd like to do a few other things with that tie."

"I'm standing here in a tie and cheap slacks because I'm waiting to take your order in one of the most expensive restaurants in Palm Beach County. You can afford to eat here, but I can't. I'd hardly say that reeks of competency. As for the tie, let all your thoughts fade away. That's not even on my radar these days."

Did I just admit to being celibate? Gah, I'm such a flake.

Not really. Drew was a well-educated, well-mannered, and wealthy man, and I was an emotionally stunted college-dropout single mom who waited tables to support our daughter and myself.

"You couldn't be further from the truth. But I'm not going to sit here and sing your praises. I'd rather whisper them in your ear on the beach, or over breakfast with our daughter."

"Listen, Drew, I have other tables. I have to get your drink order and move on." I couldn't stand there and listen to his promises—they were wishes and dreams to me.

"Club soda, lime, New York strip, medium rare, broccoli, and a glass of cabernet with my steak. Send your runner and go do your thing. I'll watch from a distance, and then I'll drive you home."

"I'll be back with your order, but you're not driving me home."

"We'll see."

I let out a long sigh and trudged off to the bar.

Tonight couldn't end soon enough.

CHAPTER 22

Drew

With my monster hangover still looming, or perhaps it was just the realization I had a kid, I nursed my second glass of cabernet while waiting for Jules to finish.

The ever-efficient "Claire" ran from table to table, checking on customers, making sure they were happy, and taking the time to smile and thank each one for coming to the Southern.

Everyone but me.

I didn't care. I was watching the woman I'd pined for over the last seven years saunter back into my life.

With hooded eyes, I watched her cash out.

"I'm done for tonight."

She ran a hand along her smooth hair until it met the bun. I wished she would take it out, but she didn't. I matched her moves, raking my hand through my own short hair.

"I didn't pay, so I guess you're not finished." I stood and reached in my back pocket for my wallet.

"I treated you to dinner—which I plan to do every time you show up in my section, or this restaurant for that matter. You can't just barge back in my life, involve my boss, and make promises to my daughter that I don't even know if you know what it means to keep them."

She turned and headed toward the door.

"Jules!" When she didn't even turn around, I shouted, "Claire, wait."

"Let her go, buddy," the manager called after me. Luckily, the place was empty except for a few employees now drinking at the bar.

"Don't tell me. You don't know," I spat back at him.

"I do know. In fact, I've known Darla since she was just a month old. I always figured she looked like her dad, but it's uncanny. So, don't you tell me what I know and what I don't know. Where have you been while I've been watching your daughter grow up?"

He shouldn't have gone there. I shouldn't have cared what he thought. My body shouldn't have filled with jealousy at his mention of knowing Darla since she was a month old, but it did.

And I punched the ever-loving shit out of Bryce.

My fist connected with his cheek, knocking him into a table, and glasses and silverware went flying. He was about to fall when I grabbed him by the throat, prepared to squeeze the life out of him.

"Drew! Drew, stop . . . let him be. He didn't do anything to you."

I felt a hand on my shoulder and released my grip.

"Drew," she whispered in my ear. "Come on, leave him."

I stood and shook my hand out. "Sorry, dude, but don't ever disrespect my daughter or me. I wasn't there then but I'm here now . . . and I'm not going anywhere."

I had to give it to the guy. He stood there with his cheek red and swollen, and stared me down.

"Then don't ever disrespect Claire again, you hear me? If you hurt her, you'll deal with me. Feel me?"

"You don't have to worry about that. Just mind your own business when it comes to my daughter." I was part caveman, part papa bear. Some innate instinct I didn't even know I possessed reared its head.

"I'm taking you home," I growled. "Claire . . . fuck it. Jules, let's go."

Her tie had come undone, and her eyes were wary. She looked mad and

. . . damn it, hot as hell. Fuck, I knew better than to let my mind go in that direction.

She stomped out of the main restaurant and practically raced for her car. When she reached for the car door, I grabbed her by the waist and hauled her toward me. Turning us until my ass was leaning on her car and she was wedged against me, I kept a tight hold on her waist.

"I don't know what I need to do," I told her, "but understand this. I'm not going anywhere. I know I have to take it slow with Darla, but let me be clear . . . I'm only going so slow for so long. I didn't know I had a family, but now that I do, I'm getting it back. For good."

When she eyed me like I was the devil, I said, "Now, come on. I'd rather you didn't work in this job, but you do, so I'm driving you home." I took her wrist gently and led her to my car.

"Drew, this is absurd. I've been doing this for six years. I don't need you to protect me, and what about my car?"

"We'll get it tomorrow when you wake up and after I go to the gym. Then we can take Darla out for pancakes."

"What about me? My life? My job? Everything I've built?"

"Life as you know it, babe, is over. What you've built on your own is awesome, but what we're going to build together is going to be even better."

It was like a fantasy, one I'd never even imagined. Yeah, I'd dreamed of fast cars and even faster women, but never a daughter.

Yet there I was, satiated like a man post-coital after I'd spent most of Saturday with the girls. I'd carried Darla on my shoulders on our way for pancakes, even though my knee was screaming at me. My heart didn't let my stupid joint win out; I was carrying my girl around. It was a high I'd never dreamed of.

My spirits soared. I was a bird, a plane, no . . . I was . . . who even cares. My life had transcended to something epic. It didn't even bother me when I tried to pull Jules close and she whispered, "No touching," as we made our way into the diner for breakfast.

I was there. With Darla. With Jules. I'd touch later.

Except Jules insisted on going to work, and someone named Molly came to watch my daughter. I'd never been so torn.

I wanted to go with Jules, but I also wanted to stay and watch this Molly character. Maybe I could run a background check, or have Sully call in a favor down at the police station.

I also couldn't allow Jules to go to work without me being there. There was that cock—her boss—and then all the men leering at her. I'd seen enough of that shit the few times I'd been there.

In the end, I went with Jules, because I knew staying with Darla would be a battle I wouldn't win.

Until next time.

Sunday morning, I worked out like I'd just won the Olympics. If you looked up *pussy-whipped pansy* in the dictionary, you'd find me with all my oversized dreams and comparisons. One minute, I was Superman, and the next I was in the Olympics.

Truth was, I'd just found out I was a dad, and was scared shitless about doing it all right.

Or wrong.

Today was the day Darla and I would start our lessons. Jules and Darla were scheduled to meet me at the club after my workout. I had a group of eight- and nine-year-old boys at ten o'clock that Darla could keep up with.

Of course she could. She was my freaking flesh and blood.

"Hi, Coach Drew," Darla chirped, knocking me out of my stupor.

"Hey, Darla, you ready?"

My daughter stood before me in crisp tennis whites. Her mom stood to the side in yoga pants and a long-sleeved T-shirt, no makeup, and messy hair.

"Yep." Darla bounced from foot to foot, her pink shoes sparkling.

"Why don't you do some jumping jacks and warm up while we wait for the others?"

"Mom said we were early, but I didn't care." She dropped her racquet on the court and jumped into a small *X* and back.

"Do twenty, and I'll be back and look at your grip." I walked toward Jules, who looked exhausted. "You okay?"

"Yep." She stifled a yawn.

"Why don't you go up to the restaurant and get some coffee? She'll be fine."

We both turned and looked at Darla, who was counting out loud.

"Fifteen, sixteen . . ."

"It's okay." Jules stared at the green concrete court.

"Done." Darla ran over and tapped my elbow. "Done, Drew!"

"Darla, tell your mom you're good down here, and she should go get some coffee."

"Yeah, Mom."

The tiny person twirled back and forth in half circles, her hair flying in the air. If looks could kill, I'd be dead by Jules.

"Let me put your hair up, Dar."

"Mom, it hurts. You pull it too tight."

Something told me I needed to back up Jules. "Darla, you have to be able to see. You're playing with the big kids, and I need your A game."

"Okay. Can you put my hair up, Mommy?"

And just like that, it was thirty–love. Me–Jules.

"Great, so go grab some coffee and a newspaper, and I'll run Darla up to the café after the lesson." Without giving Jules a chance to respond, I turned to Darla. "Let's go check out your grip."

As I finished speaking, a bunch of boys made their way onto the court, laughing and burping.

"Good morning, boys. We have someone new joining us. This is Darla."

Seth, one of the older boys, scoffed at me. "A girl?"

"Girls can play tennis too. My mom played," Darla said stubbornly, defending herself.

I bit back a smile. "It's true. Now, let's hit the baseline."

"She your cousin or something? She looks like you," Seth said.

I shook my head. "No, she's not my cousin. Now, hit the baseline or you're running suicides."

CHAPTER 23

Jules

I t was the first time in six years I'd sat in a restaurant reading a newspaper and sipping my coffee like a lady of leisure. And I was neither a lady nor a person of pleasure.

Of course, I owed it all to Drew . . . of all the fucking people.

Like my words meant nothing, as if my feelings weren't traitorous enough, my mouth had changed course and easily agreed to everything he suggested.

I smoothed my messy hair with my hand, tied it back, and closed the paper, leaning back in my chair and taking a long breath. Although I was tired, this was the best I'd felt in a long time.

I sat back up and looked at my watch. It had been an hour, so I tried to get the server's attention for my check when I spotted Drew. He was telling my server something, Darla by his side. He patted her on the shoulder and shook his head before pointing over at me.

I stood up, and they made their way toward me.

"Mom, I did great, Coach Drew said. He did."

"She did," Drew said with a grin. "Kept up with my eight- and nine-year-olds, but I'm sure you figured as much."

I nodded. "She's very skilled for her age."

"She comes by it naturally."

"Mom." Darla tugged on my shirt. "Drew said he would get me a strawberry smoothie if you would allow me?"

"Wait, let me get some money." I reached down to my purse hanging off my shoulder until a hand settled on mine.

If I weren't a grown woman with a kid, I would have swooned, physically swayed from side to side. To say our attraction hadn't waned would be putting it lightly. A slight caress of his fingers, and I was mush. Jell-O, sludge, pudding, all goopy.

"It's on me, Jules."

"My mom is Claire." Darla looked up at him with a confused expression.

"I'll explain to you later, Dar," I said, hoping she would forget after sucking down a smoothie. "Why don't you go get the smoothie? A small one, though."

With Darla tramping back to the counter, her sparkly shoes reflecting off the windows, I nearly growled at Drew. "You can't—"

"I know; I'm sorry. I want to rewind and do every day of the last seven years over. Can you understand that? I missed all of this. Even you being pregnant." His hand wrapped around mine, his thumb moving over my skin in a caress. "She's so good. God, she's a miniature you, that determined look on her face as the ball makes its way over the net."

"I don't know if being a mini-me is a compliment." I tried to move away, but as soon as I shifted back on my heels, Drew tightened his grip on my hand.

"I'd like to take you to dinner this week. Either just us or the three of us, depending on what you want. Anywhere you want. Italian, sandwiches, vegetables, whatever."

He stared me down with his blue eyes, and for the briefest of moments, I was lost at sea again. I didn't care about life jackets or maps; I wanted to be lost in him.

Drew swallowed and his brow furrowed. His fear of rejection was so palpable, my silence clearly making him uneasy, that I changed course. And just like that, my resolve to maintain boundaries went out the window.

"Yes. We should do it. I don't work on Mondays, but I'll have to see if

Molly can come. She already comes a lot, which makes me sad to leave Darla again, but I think we should do this without her."

"Do you know Molly well? I meant to ask."

"Drew, I need a sitter and I found her through Care.com. Give it a rest."

"You don't really need a sitter. I can set you up . . ."

I shook my head as Darla made her way back toward us. I wasn't quitting my job for a man. Even if he was the man of my dreams and the father of my daughter.

"Mommy, this is so good. You have to try it." Darla shoved her straw toward me.

I bent down and took a sip, feigning ecstasy. "Yum!"

"Darla, see you next week? Maybe you and your mom will have lunch with me after the lesson?"

"Yay! Can we?"

The weasel; he'd gotten a dinner and a lunch out of me in two minutes flat. I really needed to put up some boundaries.

"Darla, be careful of the straw," was all I said in response. "Thanks, Drew."

Then I took Darla's hand and hightailed it out of the posh club before I agreed to anything else.

CHAPTER 24

Drew

O n Monday, I hit the gym hard and then went to the office, avoiding any extra conversation with anyone. I was a man on a mission.

After lunch, I pondered whether to text or call Jules. A call was more romantic, but a text more pragmatic. When it came to dealing with single moms, I was starting to realize pragmatic was best.

Drew: Does tonight work? Were you able to get a sitter?

I also considered asking my office manager, Marge, to watch Darla. I knew Marge's family and where she lived. She was a nice lady, a soon-to-be grandma, a little soft around the curves, and she baked a mean brownie. Surely, she was better than this Molly.

Jules: I did. Molly can come at six.
Drew: Great. I'll pick you up around six. What is Molly's last name?

This whole being-a-parent thing was eating away at me.

Jules: Drew, let it be. See you later. Can we do something casual?
Drew: Sure thing. There's a great Middle Eastern place in town
with a lot of veggie options. Sound good? It's not fancy.

I'd prefer to take her somewhere exclusive and expensive, show her how life could be with me, but that wasn't Jules. She was nothing like the other women who had tried to worm their way into my bed to reap the fruits of my labor. Jules wanted nothing to do with my bed.

Jules: Perfect.

Forty–love, me.

I left work around five, which was a bit unusual for a Monday, but I needed to shower and change. At home, not in my office. I had to attend to other needs so I didn't blow my wad at dinner. And I didn't mean on the check.

At quarter after six, I arrived at Jules's place. I was sure she didn't want me to come up, but I did. As someone opened the door to her building, I jetted inside behind them.

Something else I'll have to deal with. Security.

"Hey." Jules answered the door out of breath, slipping a Tom on one foot and hopping on the other. "I'll be ready in a sec." She kept me at bay, only holding the door open a quarter of the way.

"Can I say hello to Darla?"

"She's in my room watching a movie." Lowering her voice, she whispered, "Let her be, Drew. This must be confusing enough to her."

"Okay."

When Jules shut the door in my face, I stepped back toward the opposite wall and leaned against the drab paint. Thirty seconds later, she came out, and I got to take in all of her.

"Ready," she said, but I barely heard her over my pounding heart.

Dark skinny-jean capris covered her legs, and a long white tank hung off her right shoulder. She'd left her hair down, and big gold hoops tangled in her messy red hair. When my gaze made its way back up to her red-glossed lips, I reached out and swiped off the gloss with my thumb.

"Sorry," I whispered, and without thinking, I leaned in and kissed her. At first, she was reluctant, but then she gave in, moving her lips along mine.

I nudged her gently back against the door, my front melded to hers, my dick seeking friction with any damn part of her. She opened her mouth to speak and barely got out a squeak before my tongue shoved its way inside. A moan rumbled up my chest.

"Drew," she finally got out.

"Yeah?" I murmured against her mouth.

"Not here," she said *after* swiping her tongue along mine.

I took that as a good sign, a promise of something more to come later. Maybe?

With a gentle closed-mouth kiss, I ended it. "I couldn't help it. I've been wanting to do that since . . . forever."

She giggled. "You're getting cheesier and cheesier."

Like magnets with opposite forces, our lips were back together. She'd said *not here*, but that wasn't what her lips were telling me. They were soft and not the least bit reticent when they met mine. She was hungry for me, and she opened greedily when my tongue sought entrance.

I slid my hand down her side, over her clothes, and back up underneath so my thumb could trace her smooth skin. I wanted her here. Now. But she was better than that. She was the mother of my child, no longer my student. Not that she ever was. She'd been my player. Whatever.

Our tongues melded and molded, a mash-up of the best kind. Moans harmonized in the hallway until I was the one who broke free.

"Any louder, someone's gonna call the cops." I placed a chaste nip on her nose.

She laughed, seeming relaxed. I liked that look on her.

I laughed back. "By the way, I'm only cheesy when I'm with you. You make my whole brain collapse into nothing." I took her hand and squeezed, pumping it over and over. "And you make my heart pound like fuck."

When she smiled and ducked her head, making her hair fall in a drape over her eyes, I brushed it out of the way. "Come on, let's go."

"You got it, King."

We went downstairs and I opened the passenger door of my car. As she slipped in, I took a moment to stare at her before shutting the door.

"This car isn't very dad-ish," she said when I slid into my seat.

"I have an SUV too."

She rolled her eyes. "Of course you do."

I winked and turned the car on, letting the engine roar to life. Whoever said German engineering wasn't the best, was wrong. Period.

"You look great, by the way." I kept my eyes on the road, but caught her sly smile in my peripheral vision.

"Thanks."

"Want some music?"

"Can we put the windows down?"

"Sure thing."

I flicked the air off and opened all the windows. The evening air was still humid, but as we entered the highway, a breeze kicked up. Jules leaned into the headrest and closed her eyes, her hair blowing all around her face.

"Like that?" My voice carried over the wind noise.

"Feels like freedom. You could give me a million bucks, and it wouldn't feel as good as this."

The burden she'd carried weighed heavy on her, but she wasn't shaming me. She was sharing with me. Somehow I knew that as well as I knew my own date of birth.

I wanted to answer, to say something profound, but I didn't want to disturb her moment. So I let it be and she stayed like that, her hair blowing furiously and her eyes at peace until we exited the freeway.

"Jules," I said, drawing her out from her languor. "I want you to know, I'm here now. Whatever small moments of freedom I can give you, you need to ask me." I stopped at a red light and turned, grabbing her hand. "You hear me?"

She nodded. "It's not easy giving up control. For the last six years, every sleepless night, every puke fest, and every glorious moment, it's only been me."

"But you can. Look how good this feels. You're practically having an orgasm from the wind blowing in your face."

The light turned green and I removed my hand to shift gears. "Imagine how good it will feel when I blow on your—"

"Drew! Don't say it."

"What?" I taunted her, enjoying the sexy smile on her face. "You're still a woman, right? Not only a mom. I'm sure you have wants and desires, and lucky for you, I know exactly how to find them. I just take the tip of my—"

"Stop it," she said over a laugh.

I liked to make fun of Jules. Her cheeks pinked every time I got a rise out of her, and it never failed to make my dick hard. Crap, I needed to adjust myself in the worst way, and this car was a stick shift and I was coming to a light.

"It's not funny. It's been a long time."

"How long?" I asked, both intrigued and hopeful.

She shook her head. "Nope, not copping to that."

I turned to the driver's side window and smirked. *Since me, I think.*

"You hungry?" I needed a quick change of subject. My body was continuing to react in ways it shouldn't when I was operating a motor vehicle.

"Yeah, I am. It was a busy day. I played catch-up. Laundry, bills, groceries, and then getting ready for this. I've actually never done this, gone out for the night. Not since Darla."

I pulled into a parking lot and shifted into park. "I'm glad you agreed. I'd like to do it with Darla too. There's this awesome ice cream parlor near the library, and a pizza place next door. Maybe we could do all of it. Oh, and there's those water fountains that kids run through."

"How do you know all this?" Jules turned and looked at me, her brow furrowed. She shoved her hair back and scooped it into a bun.

"I'm on the board at the library, and we had a meeting the Monday after I saw Darla for the first time. I couldn't think straight, so I spent some time walking in circles around the area, and everything I saw . . . I wanted to do with her."

Jules didn't say anything in response. I wasn't sure whether her silence was out of anger or surprise, but I added, "And you."

CHAPTER 25

Jules

My head hurt, actually ached at the thought that he'd spent time wanting to do all that with Darla. My body also fully lit up, although it had already been somewhat aroused during the car ride. But now it was a fiery mess. I was an asteroid burning through the sky, and Drew . . . Drew was the source drawing me in.

"That actually sounds wonderful," I murmured.

"Really?" His thumb moved back and forth over mine.

"Really."

"Good, we'll do it. First, let's eat dinner tonight." He stepped out of the car and opened my door before paying the attendant.

The restaurant was called Abba, and it was an Israeli-style bistro. The outside was fashioned in white stone like the old city of Jerusalem. I'd remembered this from a comparative religions course I took at my first college. Greenery ran alongside the wall and up the stairs toward the door.

Drew pulled it open, and we walked inside. Tantalizing scents of citrus and sesame hung in the air.

"Hi, welcome to Abba."

"I called earlier. Drew King for a table of two. Adam Sell told me to speak with Marjorie."

"I have you right here." The hostess pecked at her iPad. "Table for two by the open kitchen."

"Sounds good," Drew said, grabbing my hand and squeezing it.

"Right this way."

The place was busy. It was all windows and bright, unlike the Southern. Fresh fruits and vegetables hung over the open kitchen, and the staff wore their whites with small blue handkerchiefs tucked in the pockets.

A Middle Eastern melody filtered through speakers as we were seated directly across from the kitchen in a dark blue leather banquette for two.

"This is gorgeous," I noted.

"It's a far cry from a steakhouse."

"I was sort of thinking that. It's definitely a nice change of pace."

When the server came, Drew ordered a large bottle of sparkling water and a Scotch on the rocks. I ordered a glass of Israeli cabernet.

We made more small talk until the drinks arrived. "We're taking our time," Drew told the server, "and going to have our drink and then order."

The server hurried away, and after a clink and a toast to reunions, Drew asked the sixty-four-million-dollar question.

"When do you think you're going to let me all the way back in? In every way, Jules?" He tossed back a healthy dose of Scotch, his Adam's apple dipping with each swallow.

"Drew," I whispered.

"I don't want to make small talk. I want to talk for real. I'm sorry for what I did, pushing you away, but if I thought for a minute that all of this was about to happen—Darla, you dropping out of school, waiting tables . . . Christ." He slammed his drink down.

"Please don't cause a scene." I reached across the table and placed my hand on top of his. My fingers pressed into his skin, and tingles ran through me. "I was so broken when you left. I'd been through a mess at my other school, and I knew being with you was wrong. It was like I was binge-watching horror movies, except they were real, the mistakes of my life on a continuous loop."

He flipped our hands and squeezed my fingers tightly.

"When you up and left, it was a bold reminder of what I did was wrong . . . again."

He shook his head. "You know what happened in California wasn't your fault."

"Yes." I took a large sip of my wine. "I do, but it was like I kept putting myself in positions where I was screwing up."

"You can't seriously believe that shit."

"I don't know what I believe. When I found out I was pregnant, I decided to start over. Dropped out of school, started using my middle name, and hauled ass to North Carolina. For some reason, it was easier being all by myself. Anything from my former life reminded me of you. I can't explain it, but all I wanted was to be someone new."

"Have you been happy?" His eyes were like daggers, ready to stab the truth out of me.

"I can't really answer that. Darla makes me so happy. She's a beautiful and strong little girl, and I'm raising her all on my own, no frills. But I'm lonely a lot of the time. When Dar is asleep or at school, doing laundry or shopping isn't exactly fulfilling."

"I haven't been happy. Actually, I've been a sorry sack of shit for years. The last five years, all I've done is think of you." He picked up his glass, the ice clinking against the side, and finished off the amber liquid.

"What about the other two years?" It was a stupid question, and I should have left it alone.

"Truthfully, the first year I was pretty much drunk on the weekends or working. Then I sobered up and made several big hits while screwing my way through women. It wasn't very satisfying. They weren't you, physically or personality or anything. I took all my anger out on my body, working out until I was exhausted."

I nodded and finished off my wine.

Like I said, I shouldn't have asked. I hadn't slept with anyone since before Darla was born. Since Drew left Ohio.

"We're going to make this right, Jules. I never stopped caring for you. I already can't imagine a life without you and Darla. We'll make it right, and I hope in a few short weeks or months, you'll allow me to take care of you."

"God, I wish it were that easy." I dropped my forehead in the palm of my hand, when I really felt like slamming it into the table.

"We don't have to make this hard."

"Darla thinks her dad just couldn't be with us. It's so stupid, the rock bottom of excuses, but I could never bring myself to say anything disparaging about you," I whispered to the table.

"I get it; we'll work through it. Right now, let's eat and relax."

I looked up. "How do you know to say all the right things?"

"With you, it comes easy. Like I was meant to take care of you."

My eyes squeezed shut. Jesus, my insides were melting, all my resistance crumbling.

The server popped over, noticing our drinks were empty. "Another round?"

Drew looked to me, and I nodded. He gave the server a thumbs-up.

"Can I interest you in some food?"

"How does the tasting menu work? Can we do an all-vegetarian version?" Drew again with all the right things.

"Absolutely," the server said.

I looked at Drew. "You don't have to do vegetarian."

"I'm not," he said and turned to the server. "One tasting menu as-is, and one veggie only."

"Would you like the wine pairings too?"

"Of course. Even if we just take a few sips of each, that's what makes it."

The server disappeared, and it was as if we were the only two beings in the universe . . . despite the kitchen bubbling over with chatter and pots clanking right next to us.

"Not to take it heavy again," he said, "but I looked for you. Facebook, shit like that."

"I never got back into it. When I left, I could only afford a pay-as-you-go flip phone for emergencies. By the time I finally got a smartphone, I had a two-year-old and no time to Facebook or Instagram."

A runner deposited our drinks in front of us, along with a decadent display of hummus, baba ghanoush, pita, and olives.

"And the Claire business?"

119

"That was right away. I decided moving wasn't enough. I would be someone entirely new."

"I like Jules better." He stared me down, his gaze hungry and predatory.

"It's okay. You can use it. I should tell Darla my real name. I've kept too many secrets from her."

Drew popped an olive in his mouth, spitting the pit in a little dish meant for that exact purpose. He swept some hummus on a piece of pita, then reached over and fed it to me. I had a little buzz going, and all of a sudden realized how horny I was.

Except I had a kid at home. I couldn't exactly invite Drew over . . . could I?

The rest of dinner pretty much went the same, with Drew attending to my every need and me falling further into the palm of his hand.

After dinner, he asked, "Want to go for a drive?"

All I could do was nod. I didn't have much more to drink after feeling the tiny buzz forming.

I was lost in my thoughts as we drove. Before I knew it, we were parked at the far end of Drew's driveway, overlooking the ocean.

"I can't come in . . . or stay . . . or anything." It was a hushed whisper.

He killed the engine and looked at me. "I know. By the way, I'm paying the sitter."

I pursed my lips and tried to give him a dirty look, but couldn't seem to erase the smile from my face.

"I thought we could just look at the moon without getting arrested for loitering elsewhere. And we could . . ."

He leaned over the center console and guided me close. With his hand around the base of my neck, he kissed me. Softly, with a closed mouth, yet his kiss touched me to my tippy toes. On a moan, his tongue found entry into my mouth, and mine journeyed into his. The heaviness of earlier had fled, and all that was left was the silent promise of something better.

We stayed like that a long time, just kissing and kissing.

I wasn't a single mom, and he wasn't the man who ran away from me. We were Jules Smith and King Drew again. He was my hot coach, my savior, and I was his student and lover.

His tongue abandoned my mouth and traveled down my neck, his teeth nipping at my skin, tingling and teasing along my collarbone. His hand slid over my shoulder, moving the strap out of the way for his mouth as he bent his head and caressed my skin with his lips. I couldn't do anything but lean my head into the headrest and sigh.

It had been too many years since I'd been touched. I hadn't even considered finding a replacement for the man who held my heart in his calloused hands. And now he was kissing me, touching me, holding me, almost bringing me to the brink with light foreplay.

With his head still bent, he stopped over my heart and laid his forehead over the stammering muscle. "Jules, I needed you, craved you all these years. I'm so glad I found you."

When I breathed out his name, he released my seatbelt and scooped me over into his lap. His erection dug into my jeans, making me want to shed the heavy layer and feel him. Really feel him. Slide him into me. Orgasm with him inside me. My mind was on a crash course, going a hundred miles an hour, not caring what obstacles might or might not lie around me.

"Babe, you feel so good like this. Just like this. I've never wanted a woman the way I want you. I want it all, every piece of you, every stray hair, every inch of skin, every fiber of your being."

My heart jerked and jostled inside my chest when my phone buzzed, spoiling the moment.

I jolted up. "I have to get that. It can only be one person." Without looking at the caller ID, I said, "Hello, Molly? Is everything okay?"

"Hey, Claire. Sorry to bug you. God, I feel so stupid. This is the first time you go out for some fun, and I'm calling you."

"Please, Molly, is Darla okay?"

Drew's face turned furious in the pale light of the car, storm clouds brewing in his eyes.

"Yeah, I think so. It's just she's burning up, and I've been trying to comfort her for about an hour, but I can't seem to keep her cool or calm her down."

"I'm on my way. Did you take her temperature? There's a digital thermometer in the medicine cabinet. One second." I cupped my hand over the phone. "We have to go. Right now," I said to Drew, who had already turning the ignition and was backing out of the driveway.

"I'm back," I said to Molly, and heard Darla whimpering in the background.

"I'll take her temperature," Molly said. "I've been putting cool cloths on her forehead, and I have her stripped down to an undershirt and underpants. She's also taking small sips of water, and I found a popsicle in the freezer that she's been sucking on. I'm sorry, Claire. I really thought I could hold her off, but she's crying for you, and I can tell you're the kind of mom who wouldn't want that—"

I stopped her rambling, "It's okay, Molly. I'm glad you called. Please, just go take care of Darla. I'll be there soon."

"Okay."

I swiped the END CALL button and closed my eyes. After a deep exhale, I said, "Well, this is my life. I don't kiss boys by the moonlight anymore."

A tear escaped my eye and trickled down my cheek. I cried for how happy I'd been in that moment with Drew kissing me. Then I wept for how idiotic and selfish I was, crying over a man when my daughter was sick.

Drew didn't say a word. He let me cry, but he didn't even try to comfort me.

"This is why this isn't going to work," I told him. "Whatever you want. Dates and tasting menus. The beach and kissing my shoulder. That's not my life. Darla is my life."

"Our life," he finally said. "Our life, Jules. Not yours. You don't have to do this alone anymore. You're not going to. If I wasn't so anxious to get back to your place, I'd pull over and shake the stubbornness out of you."

I didn't respond. I couldn't.

CHAPTER 26

Drew

A beaten-down man, I collapsed on my couch.

Christ. I slammed my hand into the pillow and let my head fall back. I was such a stupid, selfish man. My daughter was sick, and I was out romancing her mother like she didn't have a care in the world.

The sad part was that Jules felt guilty about it all. I should be the one to feel guilty. Instead, I was pissed as fuck.

Jules refused to allow me in to help her. She was so frazzled over Darla being sick and her being out and having fun, so I let her go.

I shouldn't have.

After standing and pouring myself a Scotch, I moved to the patio and smoked a cigar before falling asleep in a lounge chair.

Hours later, I woke up with a stiff neck, a raging boner, and my phone vibrating in my pocket.

"Hello." My voice was ragged and hoarse.

"Oh, I'm sorry, Drew. Did I wake you?"

"Jules." I sat up straight. "It's good. I needed to get up and go to the gym anyway," I said like an idiot, looking at my watch.

It was seven in the morning. I hadn't slept in like this since I'd moved to Florida. I moved my hand in front of my eyes, shielding my aching head from the sun.

"I felt bad about rushing you off last night, and I didn't say thank you. Sometimes I forget not everyone is up at this hour."

"No, I'm always up. I just—"

My phone beeped with call waiting, and I took a quick peek at the screen. The gym. Yep, I told you; if I missed a workout, they'd be worried. I let it go to voice mail.

"Jules, you don't have to thank me. How is Darla?"

"She's sleeping. I double-dosed her with ibuprofen and acetaminophen, and that seemed to give her some relief."

"Can you do that? Double dose?" I ran my hand over my face. I didn't know shit about kids, but this was my daughter.

"Yeah, it's how to take a big fever down. I'm hoping it will break and she can go back to school tomorrow, but you never know. She could get a rash or sore throat. I guess I'll see when she gets up."

"Why don't you get some rest while she's sleeping." I opened the slider, and the air conditioning slapped me in the face as I walked back inside.

"I have to try and find coverage for work. Molly's not feeling great now either. I think by tomorrow, they'll both be better, and she'll be fine to stay with Molly. I can't take off all week."

Bingo. I hated to admit it, but I had my "in" with a sick Darla and Molly.

"I know how much you want to work, and need to. How about I stay with Darla tonight?"

"I don't know. She hardly knows you. Won't it be awkward?"

"We're going to tell her eventually I'm her father, right? Let me do this now, help take care of her. In fact, I can work from home today, and you could even bring her here. Maybe some fresh air later will do her good."

"Drew, I think it's too much."

"Jules, please." I paced my living room, begging to take care of a sick little girl like it was my last dying wish. And it was.

"Do you even know what you're doing?"

"You'll tell me." I kicked my shoes off and started undressing. Sleeping outside in the humidity had left me funky, and I needed a shower. "I'll call for groceries too. What should I get? Some broth? Applesauce?"

"And some popsicles."

"So that's a yes? What time will you be here?"

"I hope this goes okay. See you at three."

And like that, she hung up.

At quarter after three, I watched from my upstairs office window as Jules pulled into the driveway.

She looked nothing like that put-together, tight-ass server I saw the first night at the Southern. Her hair whipped around her face as she threw open the driver's door. With her shirt untucked and no tie in sight, she walked around the car and opened the back passenger door. She leaned in and helped Darla out.

I wanted to keep watching, but decided to go open the front door. I was there as soon as Jules hit the threshold.

"Hey, Darla. How ya feeling, little superstar?" I looked at my daughter standing in a pair of what I presumed to be pajamas.

"I'm fine. Mom's fussing."

Jules ran her hand over Darla's head and tucked her hair behind her ear. "Dar, if you need me, tell Drew to call me." She looked up and handed me a plastic baggie with a bottle of liquid medicine in it. "She can take another dose of ibuprofen at six o'clock. The dose is marked in permanent marker on the disposable cup."

She smoothed her hand over Darla's head. "Go to sleep later, and I'll come and get you." Turning to me, her hand still firmly planted on Darla, she said, "I'm sorry to be in such a rush, but Bryce is short-handed tonight. Apparently, a stomach bug is whipping its way through the servers."

"Go." I gently put my hand on Darla's shoulder and ushered her next to me.

Jules was halfway down the walkway and I was about to close the front door when she called back to us. "Dar, do you want me to put your hair up? I don't know if Drew knows how."

"Mom," she said weakly. "It hurts my head. I'm fine with it down."

"The fever makes her head ache," Jules explained to me.

I nodded as if I knew this shit. "Go, take a load off. We'll be fine."

She turned and walked away while shoving her hair back into a tight knot.

"You know," I told Darla, "when I knew your mommy a long time ago, she wore her hair messy. Pieces of it would fly out of her bun and she didn't care."

"Really?" Darla looked up at me with big blue eyes.

"Yep."

We stood in the foyer, staring at each other for a few beats. Both of us seemed unsure of why the other was here and what to do next.

"Come on. Want to rent a movie?" I held out a shaky hand.

"Sure." Darla stuck her small hand in mine.

"You can lie here." I pointed to the couch, not giving a rat's ass over how ridiculous it was to have a sick kid lying on a white sofa. "Let me get you a blanket and a pillow."

She plopped down and curled into a ball. "Drew?"

"Yeah, Darla?"

"Do you have some lemonade?"

"I don't. Wait . . . I have a few cans of Arnie Palmers."

"Arnees? What's that?"

"It's iced tea and lemonade mixed. You'll like it, and it'll be good for your throat if it's sore."

"It is."

I came back with a lightweight blanket and a pillow, and said, "One sec." Then I got the drink and poured it into a plastic Hafton U tumbler.

"Thanks," she whispered. "I like this pillow. It's huge."

My heart ached in a way it never had before. I wanted to rub my daughter's back and kiss away the pain. It was an instinct I didn't think had been born into me. Especially with my family—cold, removed, step-this and step-that,

126

ridiculous expectations I'd never wanted any part of.

"What type of movies do you like? Cartoons? Princesses?" I sat down by her feet, snatched the remote, and flitted through the on-demand offerings.

"Drew, Ms. Green said you look like my dad. Did you know him?"

All of a sudden, I felt like I'd been punched in the gut. Like a sad excuse for a movie, an eighties romantic dramedy . . . I was that guy.

"She did?"

"Did you know him? You have the same eyes as me."

I remembered Sully saying something about kids and their mouths; anything and everything comes out of them. Back when he said it, I disregarded it, never believing I would experience it for myself.

Well, my daughter might as well have dropped the mic. I had a kid and she had a mouth.

Even when she was sick.

"I did know him," I said, going with it. Jules was going to kill me, but I was pretty sure there was no movie to distract Darla from this conversation.

She took another sip of her drink, and then a bigger one.

"You like that?"

She nodded. "Tastes good."

"The perfect amount of sweet and not," I said with a wink.

She winked back and took another big gulp.

"Here, give it to me and I'll set it right next to you on the table." I leaned over her to set the drink down.

"How did you know him?"

Settled back in my seat, I blew out a long breath. Kids and their mouths.

"We were in school together. Your mom, dad, and I." That sounded believable.

Her eyes started to close. "He's busy with work, but he thinks about me."

"He does think about you. I know it."

She gave half a nod and fell asleep.

I sat there for a long while until I knew she was out, and then I went up to my office and grabbed my laptop.

Seated back at her feet, I worked until she woke up, hot and thirsty. It was time for some meds, so I got Darla another drink and a popsicle. And this time, we did watch a movie. Not a princess movie or a cartoon, but a funny one about a bunch of kids, a dog, and their clubhouse.

Darla giggled and laid her feet on my lap. It was the best two hours of my life.

When the movie was over, Darla said she had to pee. Drew from a few months ago would have been shocked to think of himself taking a little girl to use the bathroom, but Darla was his daughter.

And nothing feels more right.

I helped Darla up and showed her the way, waiting right outside the door for her.

"You hungry?" I asked when she came out.

"No."

"No prob. Let's go rest some more."

"Thanks. Mom keeps making me eat toast."

"Well, she's a mom. She's supposed to."

This made Darla smile.

CHAPTER 27

Jules

When I knocked quietly on Drew's door, I barely heard his footsteps approach. He opened it, barefoot and with his finger covering his lips, silently telling me to be quiet.

I'd texted three times, and each time, he reported Darla was drinking fluids and resting.

"She's asleep on the couch," he now whispered, his breath tickling my cheek when he leaned close.

We stood face-to-face in the hallway, and I wriggled my nose to take in bigger whiffs of his scent. Faint hints of Scotch and sugar wafted in front of me.

"Thank you so much. Honestly, I really don't know what I would've done. I should get her home to her bed now," I said quietly.

"I know you're going to argue." Drew stepped a little closer and put his arm around my waist. "But stay."

I tilted my head to the side and raised an eyebrow. Did he think I was born yesterday?

"Not what you think. Though, don't think I don't want you. I meant that I

129

can carry Darla up to the guest room, and you can even stay with her. It . . . it has a queen-sized bed." His voice was soft and raw, his emotions playing out in his stammer.

I didn't answer.

"No monkey business, I swear. I just hate to see you shove her in a car and back out again. Plus, you look dead tired, Jules. Let me take care of you."

"Darla will wake up so confused."

Drew brushed his lips over the top of my head and pulled me as close as I could go. Mint now mingled with the Scotch and sugar. His hardness molded to my softness, my face ghosted over his chest, and I swallowed an enormous ball of lust.

"She'll be fine. You'll be there and explain where she's sleeping. You'll explain you didn't want to move her."

His lips kept brushing against my forehead. I was practically orgasming from the faint touch, and falling asleep in his arms at the same time.

"Okay," I finally murmured, unable to handle the war between my heart and my head any longer.

"Come on. I'll show you the room, and then I'll bring Darla in."

I don't even remember collapsing beneath the down comforter, or Drew bringing Darla.

"Mommy."

I heard a whisper and felt a finger poking my shoulder.

"Mommy."

I turned in the direction of the voice and pried open my eyes. My mouth was as dry as stale beef jerky. At least, I imagined that's what it tasted like—ass.

"Hi, honey, how do you feel?" I smoothed Darla's hair back and stared at my precious little girl.

"Where are we?"

I cleared my throat; it felt like I swallowed an entire dead animal. "Drew's. You were sleepy, and he didn't want me to have to wake you." I brought the back of my hand to her forehead. "You feel cool as a cucumber. Thank God."

I couldn't help myself. I pressed my lips to her forehead, kissing the heck out of my baby girl. I took in the pale green walls and the soft breeze of the ceiling fan. The bed had a forest-green canvas headboard, and the linens must have been thousand count. My cheek felt like it was resting atop satin.

"Drew gave me Arnees to drink. It tasted good," Darla said, pulling me out of my reverie.

"What did he give you?" I sat halfway up and stared down at my rumpled work clothes. I stank like steak and grease, and I wanted to step out of the bedroom as much as I wanted a root canal.

"Arnees to drink. It had lemonade and—"

"Iced tea," I said with a smile. "Arnie's? Like Arnie Palmer?"

"Yeah," she said dreamily, lying on her pillow.

Of course, she was smitten with Drew. Forget that he was her father; he was a gorgeous hunk of man doting on her every wish—in practically a palace compared to our apartment.

"This pillow is nice. I like it," she said.

Duh. "I know, baby girl. It is."

"I like it here. We watched movies, and Drew has two toilets in his bathroom."

A bidet, I presumed, but I wasn't explaining that now. "That's good, honey. I'm glad he could take good care of you."

I swung my legs over to stand up from the bed.

"He knows my daddy."

And like that, I fell backward into the bed and squeezed my fists. I knew it was only a matter of time.

Drew always got what he wanted. Years ago, he came into my life, snatched me up as his star player, and made me his lover. Okay, he didn't make me. I went willingly. But then he exited my life at his convenience.

"Mom, are you okay?" Darla's scratchy voice pulled me out of my rage, her hand gently patting my shoulder.

As I suspected, Drew was steamrolling right back into my life. Like he'd never left.

He was my ex. Darla's father. My soon-to-be lover. He wanted it all, and wouldn't stop until he got it. A shiver ran down my spine at the thought.

"I'm okay, sweetie. He did know your dad. What did he tell you?" *God only knows.*

"He said my dad thinks about me a lot. He knows it. For sure." She twisted her rat's nest of hair around her fingers.

I squeezed my eyes shut and shoved back the tears when a knock came on the door.

"Come in," I called, and Darla popped up to meet the opening door.

There he was, in workout shorts and a T-shirt, his scorpion tattoo peeking above the neckline, carrying a tray with coffee and a can of Arnie Palmer. I remembered a time I'd been fascinated with the idea of his tattoos, and then how I'd felt when I finally ran my fingers over them.

They were meant to protect his heart. But what about mine? And Darla's?

I looked at my watch for the first time since waking up. It was nine. "Wow, I just realized how late it is."

He walked in and set the tray down on the night table. "I figured you were beat, so I hit the gym and came back."

Of course he did.

"How are you, superstar?"

"Better." Darla hopped around the room on one foot until she was next to the tray. "Can I have that drink?"

"You betcha." He winked and ruffled the top of her messy bedhead.

Then, like it was an everyday occurrence, he cracked open the can and emptied it into a plastic cup for her, and poured a cup of coffee for me, mixing in the milk.

"And for your mom, coffee."

My thanks came out more like a croak, and then I focused on my daughter. "Looks like you're off one more day, Dar. Today, you'll rest up, and then back to school tomorrow." I stood, sipping my coffee and smoothing my rumpled oxford with my free hand.

"Mom, can we get bagel sandwiches for lunch? Since I'm home?"

"Sure, sweetie. But first, let's help Drew make the bed."

"Leave it," he insisted, and I gave him a dirty look. "My housekeeper will get it."

"What's that? A housekeeper?" Evidence of the huge discrepancy between the way we lived and the way he lived came rolling out of Darla's mouth, leaving Drew without a response.

"No answer?" I said, taunting him.

Drew shoved a hand through his hair, obviously at a loss for words. "Um, Darla . . ."

"Honey, a housekeeper helps someone take care of their house when they're super busy at work. Like Drew."

"You're busy at work, Mom. Super busy." Darla took another long sip of her drink, eyeing me the whole time.

"Well, it's their job. Being a housekeeper is a job, so they get paid to do it. I don't make enough money to pay someone a good salary to do that."

"Oh." Darla's shoulders sagged while Drew's gaze flicked between the two of us. "I have to pee," she said, quickly changing subjects like only a six-year-old can.

"There's a bathroom right back there." Drew pointed toward the left of the mirror, and Darla hopped toward it and shut the door behind her.

"Still want to be a dad?" My tone was angry and ruthless, and I immediately regretted it.

"I have a lot of learning to do, I guess, but yes, I want every single second. Even the ones where I sound like an ass."

He moved closer and took my coffee, setting it aside. He smelled like sweat and strawberries . . . he must have had a smoothie. I wanted to lick him everywhere. Forget the coffee and my daughter in the adjoining bathroom.

"Let me take you for bagels and then keep Darla tonight," he mumbled along my cheek, sending goose bumps running down my arm and up my spine.

I shook my head. "I don't think so. It's too much, too soon."

"Just bagels?" He kissed my earlobe, his breath tickling my neck.

"My breath." I turned my face away from his, covering my mouth.

"Just bagels, or I'm going to kiss you."

"No, no way. No kissing." I shoved him back.

"So, bagels it is."

Darla took that moment to pop out of the bathroom and catch us still

133

sitting a bit too close, occupying each other's personal space.

"Are you okay, Mommy?"

"Yep, I'm good, but I need to go home and change. Then we can go for bagels."

"And I'm going too," Drew added.

I hoped he planned on changing too. There was no way I could keep my heart in check with him looking like that, dying to catch more glimpses of the scorpion.

CHAPTER 28

Drew

Jules stood there awkward as shit in my guest room. I knew she wanted to flee, and it was my job to make sure she didn't leave. Even with my stupid blunder over what the hell a housekeeper was, I wanted to hold on tight as hell to both of them.

I didn't try to stop her from going home and changing. But I did insist on picking them up and taking them for bagels.

The windows were down on my SUV as I pulled up outside their building, and I heard a knocking above me. Sure enough, I saw Darla pounding on the window above and waving. She came running down ahead of her mother, her hair flying around her face.

"Hey, Drew, do you know the bagel place with the huge bagel on top? It has a bite taken out of it?" She'd thrown open the door and was climbing in the backseat, Jules coming up behind her.

I thought for a second. "Yeah, I do. It's called Albert's. Is that where you want to go?"

"Darla, we discussed this—"

"It's expensive, so Mommy said I shouldn't ask. But it looks so cute with

135

the bagel on top, and I want to go so bad."

Jules frowned at me. "I'm so sorry, Drew. She's been begging to go."

I decided it was time to toss another advantage my way. "You know, Darla, I wanted to try it too, but when your mom says not to ask something, you shouldn't."

Jules had climbed up front at this point, and she lowered her head and glared at me over her shades.

"It could have been something you could hurt someone by asking, and so this is good practice to listen." And now I was a parenting expert. At least, I felt that way.

Jules apparently didn't agree. "We should go. Shouldn't you be at work?"

"I called in and said I'd be in around noon. It's been a long time since I've had a lazy morning. It's sort of agreeing with me. Plus, I have a date with a superstar." I winked at Darla and then turned toward Jules. "Is it okay if we try Albert's?" *Smooth, I know.*

"Sure."

I pulled out and headed back toward the water . . . the pricey side of town.

"Want to listen to music?" I hollered back to Darla.

When I saw her nod in the rearview, I flipped on some pop station. "She seems good."

"Kids rally. They bounce back so easily, unlike us. I can't afford to go down for the count."

"You work too hard."

Jules turned her gaze out the window and didn't respond.

A tremor ran through my hand as I set it on her knee. I knew she wouldn't want the contact in front of Darla, but I didn't care.

As I expected, she gave me the evil eye, but I didn't move my hand.

"I know you had to, but you don't have to work so hard now. I know you don't want my help, but it is my obligation."

"You need to stay in your lane," she said, then lowered her voice to a whisper. "Move off my knee, and you're pushing too much. The babysitting and sleepover were enough for now."

"It's not really babysitting when it's your own kid."

If I'd thought her earlier glare was evil, this one could kill.

136

"Shhh . . . stop. Please."

I nodded and checked on Darla, who was bopping to the song in the back. "Who is this, superstar?"

"Taylor. I love her!"

I turned it up and pretended to dance and drive.

"Drew, you're silly." Darla giggled in the back.

I popped and locked with my right arm, leaving my left hand on the wheel, and she laughed out loud. My daughter.

My fucking daughter.

Jules still glared out the window, but I could see her trying to stifle a smile.

I sat in my office after bagels and another argument with Jules. She insisted on Molly staying with Darla. I thought she could come to my office for a while and then home with me.

I was pushing, but I didn't care. Fuck it . . . this was my family.

The phone interrupted my thoughts.

"King here."

"King, where the hell you been?"

"How ya doing, Sull?"

"I'm fan-fucking-tastic, been trying to track you down for two days. That fund is going through the roof."

"Told you."

"The wife is thrilled, said I can take her away now. Europe, so I don't think I'm going to say thanks after all."

I laughed into the phone. "Take your wife away."

"Oh, so you're a softie now. What did you do, fall for someone since I last saw you at the Southern? You've been MIA."

I leaned back in my chair and propped my feet up on my desk. "Seven years ago, before I moved down here, I took a job coaching tennis. There was a girl, a player of mine, who'd been hurt badly. Some bad shit at her former school. A transfer. We fell for each other and then I ran off, thinking it was best for her."

"Damn, King, you never said anything. A player? Did you get caught?"

"No. It was only a matter of time, so I bolted. Here's the thing . . . she had a kid."

He moaned on the other end of the line. "You can't let her pin that on you—"

"Sull, if you met the kid, you'd know she was mine. Basically, my clone as a girl."

"You sure?"

"I'm sure. Sure enough that I took care of her yesterday with a fever."

"You feeling okay? Maybe you got a virus or something?"

"I'm fine."

"So, what now? You do right by the kid? Give her some cash every month or a lump sum?"

"No, I want my family. I want it all."

"I guess you need to lawyer up and get a paternity test."

I sat forward and put my face in my palms, the phone in the crook of my neck. "I can't push her on this. If I lawyer up, she'll bolt this time."

"I think taking Rosie to Europe isn't looking so bad."

I blew out a long breath. "I want to be mad at you, but I can't. I only have myself to blame here, so the shit's hit the fan. I guess."

"Nah, looks like you'll get a life at the end of it."

"I'm not so sure. By the way, don't harass anyone at the Southern anymore."

"What the hell's that all about?"

"The appetizers, the server . . . that's her. The mother of my child, you ass."

"Shit, man. You sure you're still going to take good care of my money?"

"Yeah, you're in good hands. Just watch your mouth."

"I got you."

"I'll see about that. I got to go. Talk soon."

I disconnected before he could say anything else, and spent a few hours going over numbers and answering e-mails. I managed a small handful of clients who had money to burn. They typically only reached out when we took in a big profit or stood to take a large loss, which happened sometimes. Mostly, I served a who's who of Palm Beach County from my small stucco office building.

I was used to coming and going for my workouts, leaving my competent staff to take care of shit when I was gone. Which was good, because I was going to need them over the next few months.

When six o'clock came, I showered at my office and put on a crisp white shirt and dark jeans. I still had my SUV from earlier, so I didn't bother to go home and switch cars. I went straight to the Southern and asked for a table in Claire's section.

Of course, fuckface Bryce came to greet me as soon as I finished speaking with the hostess.

"Hey, man, is Claire cool with you being here?"

"She most certainly is. Spent the night at my place last night." She was going to be pissed as hell over that little zinger. Fuck her rules.

Bryce held up his hands, palms out. "No need to get in a pissing match. I'm just looking out for Claire and her girl."

I lowered my voice. "My girl."

"Yeah, it's sort of hard to miss that little fact, but where've you been?"

"Stay out of it, man. I'm here now."

We had a two-second staring contest, and he was the first to look away.

"Right, so now that all the chitchat is over, can I go see my other girl?"

He nodded. No freaking way was he going to get one over on me.

"Amanda, please see Mr. King to table forty."

"Of course." She smiled, looking me up and down.

I gazed beyond her, looking for Jules. She was standing at a large table, smiling as she took an order, her formfitting white shirt outlining her tits. As the hostess walked us past Jules, I paused next to her.

"Good evening," I said to her but looking toward her table, being the ever-friendly businessman.

She didn't even turn my way, only muttered, "Good evening."

We'd have to do something about that.

Seated at table forty, I made myself comfortable.

A few moments later, she appeared next to my table and crossed her arms over her chest. "I'm starting to think I would've been better off leaving you with Darla."

My hands on the table in front of me, my heavy steel watch weighing down my wrist, I raised my eyebrow at her greeting and demanded, "Come close."

She rolled her eyes. "Seriously?"

"Come close, Claire." This time, she leaned in without arguing.

"After you take my drink order, I want you to text Molly and tell her I'm going to double her hourly rate while she stays late. Extra late. Because I'm going to take you home, and hope to fucking God I can wait until we get there to f— To screw . . . your brains out. I've had enough cat-and-mouse, and now I'm done playing."

I'd decided this all on my drive over. I was a man, one who was used to being in control, and I was finished with all the chasing.

Jules's eyes burned emerald, but she didn't say a word.

"As much as I'd love to be with Darla, it's our time this evening. I want you, and I'm done waiting. So get me a Scotch and hurry up with all your other people."

"Drew." She was still leaning close, her dark green tie tucked between two buttons of her shirt, her nipples hard beneath her bra and shirt.

"Go. Scotch. Serve your tables, and then get ready to leave. And keep the tie on."

She turned on her heel and went. She'd always liked my dominant side, and it was high time I took charge.

I sipped my Scotch and ate grilled sea bass while I waited. No need to be too full.

When I saw her close out her last table, I picked up my check, paid it, padded it with a thousand dollars cash, then stood and handed the leather folder to Jules.

"Let's go." I took her hand and didn't wait for any answers or grumbling.

I led her to the back room so she could grab her shit, then ushered her to the back door, out the exit, around the building to my SUV, and opened the door.

"Get in."

She dug her heels in. "You can't boss me around like this, King."

"I can and I will."

140

"What about my car?"

"You'll get it in the morning. After I take Darla to school."

"I have to go home tonight."

"Get in the car. You'll go home later. I'll come back after the gym and take Darla to school, and then drive you to your car. Do I have to spell everything out?"

"Yes, you do. This is my life, and you're trying to orchestrate it."

"Exactly. Until I get what I want, then you can boss me around all you want."

She slid into my car—finally.

"What do you want?" she asked as I settled into the driver's seat.

"Everything. All of it. You and Darla, 24/7."

When I gunned the engine, she yelled, "Drew!"

"What? I want it all."

"Not that. This." She waved the money in the air.

"Better put that in your purse."

She pouted and crossed her arms over her chest.

"Be mad," I said with a huge grin. "I'm going to fuck it right out of you."

CHAPTER 29

Drew

pulled into my driveway and didn't bother with the garage. After throwing the car into park and turning off the engine, I said, "Let's go."

My body was raging. I was done. Overcooked. Fried. Baked. Burned. Whatever cliché you wanted to call it, I was it.

"Drew." Her voice was a whisper as she sat still in her seat, the passenger door slightly cracked open, and her lip trembling in the moonlight.

"Jules, listen, I didn't mean to be so forceful." Regret washed over me as a lump formed in my throat.

"It's not that." She stared out the windshield at my house looming ahead of us—either an island of pleasure or a monument of regret. "I get that was our thing. You were the coach, and I was the pupil. It was hot and sexy back then. Now too, if I'm honest. But I have Darla, and I know keeping her from you was my choice. I had my reasons but my brain is so clouded right now, I can't even remember them."

She twisted her hands together, wringing out all the tension and hopefully keeping all the hope. "What I'm trying to say is this . . . I have a life, one that I made. It may not be as glamorous as yours, but you can't throw money and demands at me like I'm some two-bit hooker."

At her words, I was heartbroken. "No, no, no. You're not some . . . I can't even say the word."

"Hooker."

"That's not how I meant to make you feel, Jules. It's just you're smoking hot, and in a way I can't even understand, you're even more attractive now that you're the mother of my child. And I'm only a dude at the end of the day. I know it's a lousy excuse, but I wanted to be with you so badly."

Her hand tangled with mine.

She was comforting me.

I was such an ass.

"Do you want me to take you home?"

She shook her head slowly. "No. But I don't want you to leave me tips, okay?"

"All right, but I need to make up for all the years I missed and you scrounged. Will you let me?"

Her hand rose to my cheek and she slid it down to my jaw. Staring into my eyes with the moonlight streaming through the windshield, she asked, "Can't you just set up a college fund?"

"Of course," I muttered. Unable to stop myself, I pressed my lips to hers. I kissed her softly, like a woman of substance, not a two-bit hooker.

I broke free and pressed my mouth to her forehead. "But she'll probably get a tennis scholarship."

"Oh God."

"She's good, Jules."

"Yeah, I know."

My mouth ghosted over hers again. "I loved you back then. Never stopped. If you need me to slow down, I will."

"No." Her lips slid along mine. "Let's go inside."

I led her through the house and to the back deck. "Sit. Please sit." I pointed toward the lounger.

She lay back and kicked off her shoes. I sat at her feet, running my hand down the length of her right foot and up the left, and she closed her eyes. I pressed my thumb into her arch and she moaned. I dug deeper, adding pressure.

"Feel good?"

A louder moan. "I may orgasm like this," she said, her eyes closed and her lips parted.

I kept working at her feet, caressing and adding pressure in intervals. Finally, coming to a stop, I said, "You work hard. I want to take care of you."

Shifting up her side, I lifted myself on top of her. Then, bracing my weight on a forearm, I made love to her mouth.

Her hips rose to meet mine and my pelvis ground into her, both of us seeking friction. My tongue traced a path down her neck, to her clavicle and back. A faint trace of her perfume still lingered, even above the smells of the night, and I inhaled harder.

Her hand batted my nose away, her middle still keeping close contact with mine. "I probably smell bad."

"You smell fantastic. Downright edible." The words fell out of my mouth as I bit her neck.

"Maybe I should shower?"

I unbuttoned her shirt and slid my greedy fingers inside, running them over her bra. But they were more than greedy, they were downright grabby, and I couldn't help but push her cup down. Her nipple puckered in the nighttime air, and I squeezed it.

"Mmm," Jules whimpered.

I let my head fall forward, and circled the same exposed nipple with my tongue.

Another hum came from her as she slid her fingers under my shirt and up my spine, leaving small shivers in her wake. Her delicate touch followed its course back down to the edge of my shirt and tugged. Breaking free from her nipple for a moment, I lifted my shirt off.

"What are you doing to me, Drew?" Her nail traced my old prep school crest.

"Making you feel good. Better than good."

My hand was working with a mind of its own and decided to unbutton her pants. With one quick flick of a button and the slide of a zipper, I slid my fingers inside. She was wet and warm, and ready for me. I traced her satin panties with my index finger, pushing inside the soft fabric.

"Before the second round," I whispered in her ear, and swirled my finger over her most sensitive part.

"Oh my . . ."

She was seconds away from coming apart, with her pants still on, and I only had one finger touching her . . . not even inside her.

"Let's do this right." I pulled my finger away to a whimper and used my hand to slide her pants off. She lifted her ass for me to make quick work. Rinse and repeat with her thong. Then I was on my knees at the side of the chair, my bad one screaming at me.

Ignoring every protest my battered body gave me, I put my hands under her and my mouth to her core. Sweeping my tongue up and down and up again, landing where my finger had been. It didn't take long—a few swipes and nips—and Jules was putty in front of me, her shirt flapping in the breeze, revealing the outline of her hardened nipples against her sheer bra. I licked and caressed her throughout the waves until her ass stilled in my hands.

Then I stuck my hand in my pocket, took a condom out, shoved my pants the fuck down, and sheathed my commando self.

Jules watched me, the amber light of the porch lamp highlighting her need-filled green eyes.

"It's okay?" I asked, setting a knee down on the lounger and leaning over her.

"Yeah, more than okay."

I gripped my length and ran it along her, wetting the tip, and I was in.

"Is this okay?" she whispered through heavy breaths.

I stilled. "Babe, what's wrong?"

"It may be different. After a baby . . ."

With my mouth over hers, I let her know nothing was different, only better, as I rocked deep inside her until we were both fully satiated.

For the moment.

We lay together afterward, her tucked into the crook of my arm, the ocean lapping in the background and the air ripe with humidity. A slight breeze swept over our bare legs, and I felt a shiver run through her body.

"You okay, Jules?"

"Yeah, it's so peaceful here. I'm not sure I've been this relaxed in the last seven years."

I pressed my lips to the top of her head and lingered, afraid to break contact, not wanting to interrupt this moment of truth. "I hope soon you'll do this all the time."

"Drew, slow down. We need to go slow. Slower than slow."

My fingers ran a lazy pace up and down her arm, and her hand smoothed circle eights over my forearm. "Would taking a weekend off and spending it with me be too fast?"

That earned me a pinch.

"I have to go home. Darla will be up for school in a hot minute and want me to leave her hair a holy mess."

"She's a lot like you when you used to wear that crazy bun."

"That was ages ago."

"I don't think . . ."

She sat up and her shirt fell open, exposing more of the creamy flesh I wanted to run my hands all over.

"What about the shower?"

She snagged her thong and pants and stuffed her lean legs through the holes. I'd never felt such panic as what was coursing through my body in that moment.

"At least a rain check on the shower?"

This got me a laugh. "Maybe," she teased, her eyes sparkling in the dim light.

"Whew." I stood and held my hand to my chest. "No joke, my chest hurt when you stood to leave."

She cocked her head to the side and examined me, her lips set in a straight line. "Really?"

"Yes. It hurt."

Closing the distance, I wrapped my arm around her middle and held her tight. Her oxford was still unbuttoned, and I buried my head in her chest. Not with sex on the brain, but because I needed to feel her heart beat.

"I didn't mean for it to hurt. I just need to get back. This feels so decadent, like a vacation. If I don't go now, I'll never leave."

With a small kiss above her cleavage, I said, "Would that be so bad?"

Silently, I snagged my shirt and vowed to myself that moment would come soon. The moment she never wanted to leave.

CHAPTER 30

Jules

The next morning, I held my lips a little longer on the top of Darla's head when we got to the school's steps. With only a few hours of sleep and my emotions in overdrive, I ached for my daughter. I'd done wrong by her. Wrong by Drew too.

Now it was my turn to make it right, and I couldn't rush. No matter how hard Drew pushed.

"I have some good news." I tugged on the ponytail Darla had begrudgingly allowed me to fix.

"Yeah." Her smile was wide and energetic.

"I'm going to work lunch and pick you up afterward, then be with you all night!"

"But you don't like working lunch, Mom."

"For you, I do. Here's a note for your teacher. You're going to stay at the afterschool program until I can pick you up. It won't be long."

"Can we go to the park and hit tennis balls?"

"Of course." I kissed her cheek and sent her on her bouncing way.

It was going to be a multiple-shots-of-espresso kind of day.

After school drop-off, I did a yoga tape, trying to center myself and my thoughts. It didn't help much; my mind kept drifting to Drew every time I bent over in downward dog. Twisting, turning upside down, none of it helped ease the ache in my heart or slow the rollercoaster in my head.

I turned on the shower and undressed while waiting for the water to heat up. Standing in front of the full-length mirror on the back of the door, I tried to look at myself through Drew's eyes. My legs were still lean and firm, mostly from working and the tiny bit of yoga I sneaked in. I had a small tummy pouch from Darla. Not huge, but my stomach wasn't flat like it was years ago. My breasts were still smallish. Carrying trays kept my arms toned.

I guess it wasn't so bad. He seemed not to notice anything different as he sank into me the night before.

I stepped into the shower and let the water rain over my hair and shoulders, grateful to be washing off work from the night before. Although I wished I didn't have to rinse Drew off my skin. His smell kept me company as I slept for a bit last night, and I liked it way more than I cared to admit.

It brought memories back of a hopeful Jules, one who believed everything would be fine between the coach and her. It had been a silly wish, especially after what had happened at my first school.

Maybe that's why Drew didn't care what I looked like now? I'd always been damaged goods to him.

Did he have some rescue fantasy? Was that all it was about with Darla?

My mind ran marathons while I washed my body. The possibilities were endless, according to my overactive brain.

By the time I'd dried off, dressed for work, and barely swallowed some food, I'd convinced myself Drew and I were headed absolutely nowhere.

"Hey, Claire, can I see you a second?"

Bryce caught me at the end of my shift when all I wanted to do was rush off to grab Darla. He'd been the one constant in my life, aside from her, and I owed him a lot.

"Sure," I said.

"What's new?" he asked as I entered his cramped office and leaned against the wall opposite his desk.

"For starters, I didn't mind working lunch. I get to spend the whole night with Darla."

"That's definitely news to me."

"Don't get excited; I'm not planning on doing it often. But it's kind of cool now that Darla is turning into a real person, a little one, but still it's awesome to just hang with her."

"I'm sure. You've done a great job with her. I love seeing it."

"Thanks. Was there something you needed?"

Bryce and I had shared a drink after closing numerous times. We'd caravanned from Carolina to Florida, had even scoped out some brunch places and playgrounds with Darla in tow around our old location. But this was beginning to feel oddly personal.

"Well, it seems like Mr. King is joining us frequently and always taking a table in your section. I wanted to make sure you know what you're doing. To be sure you're okay."

I crossed my arms over my chest. "I didn't ask him to come eat here. He does live in this town, and I guess he likes it here."

My hackles were up. I really didn't like where this was going . . . or not going. Whatever was happening was making me incredibly uncomfortable.

"Yes, I'm not blaming you. I just wanted to make sure you were okay with it, and see if you need me to intervene."

"Why would you intervene? He's paying money to eat here, and tipping me too, if that's what you were wondering."

"I didn't mean to offend you, Claire."

"Jules."

"What? What do you mean?" He leaned forward on his desk.

"My name is Juliette. Claire is my middle name. Before I met you, I went by Jules, but I changed it to keep Drew from finding me. I mean, Claire Smith? Can you get any blander than that?"

This time he rocked back in his chair, eyeing me as I checked the time on my phone. All I wanted to do was pick up Darla.

"So, that's why no Facebook?"

"I hate dredging up old business, which is why I don't. I took down all my social media before meeting Drew for other reasons, and I never saw a reason to do it again. It's a pain in the ass, and I don't really like people all up in my business."

I raised an eyebrow at him. *Like you are right now.*

"What do you prefer I call you?"

"Like I said, I'm going to go back to Jules. Maybe I'll tell Darla today, if I ever get out of here."

"And Mr. King? I assume he knows."

"I understand you're protective, Bryce, but I need to be in charge of my own life. I'll handle Drew how I see fit. And unless it interferes with my job, I don't think it's any of your concern."

On that note, I waved good-bye and stormed out of Bryce's office. Sure, we'd had arguments—over shift changes and schedules, or his firing of an innocent line cook—but it had never gotten personal before.

My head hurt thinking about all the possibilities of *why now?*

I'd looked forward to a fun afternoon. It didn't seem like that was on the menu.

Twenty minutes later, I hurried into the after-school-care classroom. "Hey, sweetie."

Darla looked up from a picture book. She was snuggled in a huge purple-and-green bean bag, studying a book on puppies, and looked content. For the first time today, relief flooded my body. She was doing okay.

Darla waved and ran to put her book back on the shelf before hugging me tightly. "Hey, Mom."

"Ready?"

She nodded, grabbed her tiny pink backpack, and said, "'Bye, Ms. Price."

Ms. Price said good-bye, smiling at me, and went back to helping a group of boys with a puzzle.

I was loading our racquets into the trunk when my phone rang. I debated answering it, but it was *him.*

Shoving my basket of tennis balls to the side, I said, "Hello."

"Hey, it's me."

"I know."

"What are you doing?"

"I'm getting ready to take Dar to play tennis," I said into the phone, standing under the shade of the trunk lid. If only it could protect my emotions.

"Oh, great. You should go to Rocky Brook."

I slammed the trunk closed. "I can't, and you know it. I'm not some kept woman or secret that you have to fund. *Now.*"

"I know," he said calmly. "You're the mother of my child. I get it. I may have to keep saying it. That's my punishment."

"What? That you have a child?" I squeezed my eyes shut and willed the phone call away.

"I didn't mean it like that. What I meant was having to keep explaining to you that you're not a burden or an unnecessary responsibility. I want to do it all for you and Darla. *Want.*"

Smothered in shame, I apologized. "I'm sorry, it's just—"

"I know. Never mind all that. Where are you going?"

"To the park. Sunnyscape."

"I'll meet you there."

"Drew—" I started, but Darla knocked on the window.

"See you soon."

And that we did. Drew came sauntering down to the courts in a pair of light gray shorts and a white T-shirt, snug and fitted. His tanned legs looked more and more delectable with each step, his quads flexing. I was pretty sure his ass looked amazing too; I just couldn't maneuver to sneak a peek from behind.

"Drew." Darla ran over to him. "Mommy worked lunch so we could play. Want to see?"

"Absolutely, superstar."

"Mom, let's do the volleys." She ran back to the service line and stood in a squat with her racquet steady in front of her face.

I wasn't sure how I proceeded to hit lobs in the air for her with shaky hands and a swarm of butterflies in my belly, but I did. Each time, her racquet made contact with the ball, dropping it where it should go, and her eyes widened with delight.

Drew clapped and brought his fingers to his mouth, letting out a loud whistle.

From afar, we were a Rockwell painting on a fall evening. Up close, we were nothing close to that.

I used up all the balls from the cage I kept in the trunk. Drew watched every single one, never interrupting or lending advice.

When it was Darla's time to pick up the balls, I walked over to the side of the court and grabbed my water bottle.

"You know who's looking hot out there?"

I couldn't stop the smile from spreading across my face.

"That's right. You." He leaned close and breathed the words into my ear on a whisper.

"Stop. I'm blushing. It's like you're the big bad coach again."

"We should play later this week. You'll kick my ass. Between the age difference and my knee, I don't even know why I'm offering."

"I'm sure you'll have the advantage." Except I didn't know if I was talking about tennis anymore.

"Let me come home with you now," he said quietly, leaning close.

"I don't think that's a good idea."

"Why?" He pushed an errant hair behind my ear, his eyes focused on me, his breath minty, his true feelings on display.

"Because I can't have sleepovers with Darla."

"I'd hardly call me a sleepover, Jules."

"I never even brought a man to the house on a date or otherwise, and you expect me to start doing that now? Sleeping with you in the room next to hers?"

"Fuck yeah, but not really sleeping. We'd be quiet, of course."

"Drew . . ."

"I'm worming my way back in, in every way possible. Doing it right this time. No running, no cutting corners, no hiding."

"I've been getting that, but this is too much. Darla will be confused."

Drew turned to Darla where she picked up the balls. "Hey, Dar, want to go for pizza and ice cream?"

"We had dinner already. Mom made sandwiches before we came here," my daughter yelled back.

"So? A slice of pizza won't kill ya. Call it a late-night snack. That's what people do in college."

"Yay!" Darla jumped in the air, and all the tennis balls she'd collected rolled off her racquet face. "Oh no!" She stomped her foot and pulled her hair free, watching the balls scatter.

"Hurry up and pick them back up," I yelled over the net.

"I'll help, then we get our pizza faster," Drew chimed in. "And then I can have time with your mom," he whispered before rushing off.

That's how we ended up sitting outside on a picnic bench, his hand on my knee as Darla washed off the stickiness and jumped out her remaining energy in the fountain. True to his word, Drew took us for pizza and ice cream—the places he mentioned on our failed date.

Over pink bubblegum ice cream, I gathered my courage and said to Darla, "You know, Dar, Claire is my middle name. My real name is Juliette."

"Oh, it sounds like a princess, Mommy. *Juliette.*" My name came out in a reverent hush.

"So when Drew and I knew each other, he called me Jules. I started using Claire when I was a grown-up, but he still wants to call me Jules."

The irony didn't escape me. I'd very much been a grown-up when Drew had knocked me up. At least, I'd thought so.

"Maybe Drew'll call me Katherine? Like my middle name? What's your middle name, Drew?" She had a million questions about names and middle names. To my relief, she was completely unfazed by the name discrepancy.

Now the library loomed against the skyline, and laid out at the bottom of the steps were those water fountains that shoot up from the ground. Darla was soaked all the way through her clothes, her hair sticking to her cheeks. She was an absolute mess and loving it.

Seeing her made my heart beat faster, and guilt swept up my spine. I wanted this for her; I'd kept this from her.

I was so wrapped up in my own emotional breakdown, I didn't even bother to move Drew's hand. I couldn't be bothered with the spectacle he was creating in front of Darla. I was too concerned with what would happen when he ran—again.

Was Darla's current state of happiness worth the risk?

"Mom, look!" She hopped on one foot through the water, her shorts absolutely sopping. She smiled and laughed and leaped again, the whole time flirting with her father. She was smitten with the very man who could make all her dreams come true.

Or not.

CHAPTER 31

Drew

"She's out cold," Jules whispered as she entered the kitchen, catching me in the middle of opening a cheap bottle of cabernet I'd found in the cabinet. "Oh, I'm so sorry. I didn't offer you a drink when we came back. Glad you made yourself at home."

"This is for you." I tipped the bottle in her direction.

She leaned back against the counter and stared at me. "I'm not sure what to make of you being here. This is all new for me."

"What? Someone taking care of you? You should get used to it."

I located a wineglass and filled it halfway with the burgundy liquid.

"I don't need a caretaker," she said as I handed over the glass.

"I'm not suggesting that. Taking care of you is a want, not a need, when it comes to me."

"It's just—"

"No more justs or buts or becauses. Drink your wine. Go sit down, relax." With my hand on her lower back, I led her to the sofa, then urged her to sit.

"I'm so afraid you're going to run again," Jules whispered into her glass.

"I'm not." I knelt in front of her. "Not. Going. To. This kneeling thing's becoming a habit. You need to understand, you're my goddess. The queen to my king."

"Oh my God, Drew. Be serious. You know I don't get into that cheese."

I bent and ran my nose down her thigh, scenting her skin and memorizing her musk.

"We have to be careful. Because Darla—"

"No more becauses, remember?"

My lips found hers and quieted all the reasons about to spill from her mouth. I was done with them, reminding myself she was a grown woman now and could take the heat from me. She wasn't a scared student. She hadn't recently been burned by her teammates.

"You've taken life by the horns—to borrow a trite expression—and steered yourself in the right direction." I bit down on her lower lip and sucked in her essence. "You found your way toward me. I don't think it was luck. It was meant to be, and now it's my job to keep you here and happy. To help you map out the future." I whispered the words into her ear and let them sink in while my thumb caressed her cheek.

Relieving her of the glass, I brought it to her lips so she could sip, and then I set it on the side table.

"I love you," I said firmly, my hands holding her face toward me, my eyes laser-focused on hers. It wasn't a sentimental moment. It was grave and serious. She needed to understand this. "And I loved Darla before I knew she existed. Now I can't breathe without her. Or you."

Jules's eyes filled with tears, and I watched her swallow. Hard.

"You feel me? You get what I'm saying, Jules?"

She nodded.

Our mouths fused again, our kiss not ending until our lips were bruised and raw.

I took her hand in mine and led her to her bedroom. It was the smaller room, I noticed, and hated that for her. Darla had the larger bedroom, complete with a toy chest and a kid's desk, but a double bed against the wall was all that adorned Jules's room.

Inside the dark room, I closed the door. "Is this okay?"

She nodded again.

"You can hear Darla?"

"Yes." Her voice was raw with emotion.

I slipped my hands behind her head, releasing the bun and letting her hair fall free. My lips were drawn to her neck; it was a pull stronger than the one that controlled the ocean outside.

"Jules," I said softly, turning her and pressing her back into the door. Taking my time lavishing the smooth skin along her collarbone, I touched the tip of my tongue to each goose bump.

Greedily, I snatched her shirt over her head, my lips leaving her skin for a millisecond, and then they were back on her. Kissing, sucking, laving.

I couldn't get enough, rock hard, coming out of my skin with want.

My hardness pushed its way toward her slight softness. My erection met her belly—the same belly that had carried my daughter. At the thought, my desire reached an all-time high.

"Take me to bed," Jules murmured.

She didn't have to beg.

Gently, I guided her to the mattress and spread her out in front of me. I bent and ran a hand up her calf, over her thigh, and into the back of her shorts, unable to deny myself a quick squeeze of her ass cheek. She laughed and squirmed enough for me to shimmy her shorts down. They were the kind with the panties attached, so Jules now lay in front of me, naked and pure.

"Too many clothes on you," she whispered.

I shoved my legs free and lay down on top of her, careful to keep my weight on an elbow. With my free hand, I ran my length along her wetness. I wanted to slip inside, no barriers—literally and figuratively.

"Please," she moaned.

"What?" I kissed along her cheekbone.

"I want you." A shiver ran through her body as she spoke.

"Let me take care of you first."

"Later. I want to feel you now."

"I need to grab a condom."

"I'm clean, on the pill. We already had an oops; the odds are in our favor."

"I want you so bad," I said, my words humming from my chest.

"Take me."

And I did. Guiding myself into her heat, I felt at home for the first time in seven years. Taking my time, I stilled at the feel of myself filling her. "Oh God, Jules."

We rocked together slowly until the friction wasn't enough.

Her feet found my ass and dug in, and I plunged deeper, harder. Our mouths fused, her nipples rubbed against my chest, and my thumb found her sensitive spot.

As she began to shake, my heart pounded heavy against my breastbone. It was the hottest missionary I'd ever experienced.

With another thrust of me in and out of her, Jules came. I rode her waves slowly, drawing each tremor out of her until her breathing steadied. Then I picked up the pace again until I could do nothing but succumb to my own climax.

Jules

"Let me get a warm towel and clean you," he whispered into my ear, and slid out from me.

I already missed him. There was an immediate hollowness where he'd been. I hadn't made love in seven years, and now after two times with this man, I needed to be filled.

I loved it.

I hated it.

I wanted it.

I despised needing it.

My head hurt and my blood pumped with a vengeance. This was exactly what I'd spent years trying to avoid. Needing someone, being dependent on another person—emotionally.

Yet my body insisted I grab onto this man; I'd dreamed of him for years. Every time I closed my eyes, his image filled my every thought.

I heard him banging around in the bathroom and wondered if I could hide under the bed. My hand found my hipbone, and then my empty core dripping from him, weeping for more, and I was instantly disgusted with myself. Having come completely undone within weeks of Drew worming his way back into my life, I pitied myself.

My thoughts were as rumpled as the quilt underneath me.

"Hey."

He was back, wiping me clean, drying me, kissing me, and loving me like I'd imagined so many times. Lingering touches along my skin triggered my nerve endings.

Physically, I wanted more.

My overactive brain wanted my mouth to scream *stop*, but my heart wouldn't allow it.

"Come here," he said, and I did.

I crawled right up to him in my stupidly small bed with the pink quilt and lavender shams. Darla had loved both when we saw them at the secondhand store. I couldn't say no to her clapping and jumping—the same way I couldn't deny her father.

"It's going to be okay, Jules. Let yourself fall. I can hold us both; I can brace your fall. I even have enough room for three in my arms."

My entire body shook and shivered at the idea of it.

He kept muttering these sweet nothings until I must have dozed off. I vaguely remembered waking up in the middle of the night when Drew unlatched the door and left it slightly ajar.

"In case Darla needs you," he said softly.

Then I drifted off again, dreaming of his home and Darla settled in his guest bed, but in my dream, it was her very own room. She was drinking iced tea mixed with fresh lemonade, and petting a turtle. Drew was walking around the house shirtless, his tattoos on display for the world to see, but instead of the crest there was a different one that read DARLA inside a heart. I was barefoot and pregnant again, this time with my feet laid up on a pillow—not working forty hours a week at a shit job.

I woke trembling and chilled.

I had to get the hell out of here. He'd left years ago—was his word really worth trusting?

No.

He hadn't been strong enough back then. He ran faster than I could say *I'm pregnant*. Forget that I never even tried to tell him.

This wasn't going to work. I needed my control back. Hadn't I learned my lesson years ago when it had been stripped from me . . . twice . . . first by my former teammates, then by Drew when he abandoned me.

I liked when the ball was in my court. The advantage was all me, or as they say in tennis, "*Ad in.*"

Not out.

CHAPTER 32

Jules

After years of playing Claire, dutiful server, I knew exactly how to play the role of *happy-go-lucky the morning after.* I pasted on a smile and drank my coffee with Drew watching me over the rim of his mug. Darla seemed as unfazed over the sleepover as she did about learning my real name.

I let Drew take her to school. He didn't know it, but it was a parting gift.

"We're going to tell her soon," he whispered in my ear as he went out the door.

Not if I have anything to do with it.

As soon as he was gone, his SUV pulling out of the lot, I called Bryce claiming to be sick. Then I packed up our belongings and transferred them to my car, shoving most in the trunk and front seat. I left the furniture. Most of it had been there when we moved in anyway.

When it was time to pick up Darla at school, I pulled my fully loaded sedan up next to the sidewalk and beckoned her with a wave and a smile.

"Hey, Mom. Drew went to work."

"I know, sweetie."

"Is Molly coming tonight?" Darla asked from the backseat, the disarray around her going unnoticed.

"We're going to take a quick trip tonight. It'll be fun," I lied.

"What? What about school?"

"You can miss a few days, Dar." Clearly, I hadn't thought a damn thing through. I dreamed up the words, serving them up like dessert. "I've missed spending time with you since the summer and being busy with the move."

"Oh," Darla said with a smile. I had her at *I missed you*. "Is Drew coming?"

"No, sweetie."

Turning onto the freeway, I went over my bank account in my head. I turned up the pop music and planned the next few days. I would tell Bryce I was still sick through the weekend. Darla and I could spend a long weekend in a motel, maybe near Jacksonville. I could scout out a diner job, where I could work days and be home at night. Make a lot of tips and keep myself under the radar.

"Why? I like Drew, and I have my clinic this weekend with the boys. I'm tougher than them. That's why Drew calls me a superstar."

It had been five minutes, and all my daughter talked about was Drew. I was pretty sure he was sitting in his office dreaming about her. Just her. Not me. If I wasn't careful, he'd take her away from me.

Defeat rained over my plan and me. I knew it was flawed. I knew he would seek me out; nothing would stand between him and Darla. Yet I kept my foot on the gas. I had to follow through.

I was a desperate junkie trying to get clean and running away from their dealer.

I needed the space. He needed to understand that.

I needed strength and direction. He should have seen that.

I needed him. He didn't need me.

He'd been the one to leave the first time.

Drew didn't get to waltz back in at his leisure and take over the life I'd built. It might be small, but it was mine.

Drew

"What the hell do you mean, she's not working tonight?"

I loomed over the hostess, who was backing away from me as fast as she possibly could on her sky-high heels.

"She's sick."

"What?" My words were getting louder.

I'd texted Jules a few times when I left work and didn't receive an answer. I thought it was because she was busy with work. Now I felt like an ass, and sadly, this hostess was in the wrong place at the wrong time.

"That's all I know. Bryce said she was sick and we were short staffed."

"Where is he?"

Like manna from heaven, the ass appeared out of nowhere.

"What the fuck? Jules is sick?" I pulled out my phone and checked to see if she'd answered any of my texts.

"That's what she said," Bryce answered, clearing his throat.

"When?"

"Early this morning, she called me. Sounded fine over the phone, but something's been going around."

"Damn it." I didn't bother answering the douche.

Turning on the heel of my Pumas, I headed toward the valet stand and jumped in my car, which was still parked out front. With a five thrown out the window, I sped out of the lot and toward Jules's apartment, knowing the whole time she wouldn't be there.

It was my fault. I'd pushed too hard, and she was pulling away.

But this time, she didn't get to keep my daughter from me.

"Jules!" I banged on her door and got nothing.

I fucking knew it.

Defeated and destroyed, I went back to my place. My throat was so constricted with emotion, I didn't even think I could swallow a drink.

I ripped off my dress shirt, the buttons popping off and flying around the room, leaving me in a white undershirt. I tossed off the shirt, shoved out of my jeans, and walked to my room in nothing but my bare ass. Bypassing the kitchen, I didn't even set the alarm.

My bed beckoned me, but I couldn't sit on it. If I did, I would think of her in my arms the night before.

I pulled a chair to the window and sat with my head leaning against the glass, watching the ocean lap against the shore. Over and over and over.

Like us, the water kept finding the sand. I had to believe we would meet again.

I ran my hand over my head. My hair was shorter than back then, but my heart was bigger. The idea of Jules had never left my heart. She'd been the standard since I met her.

And now there was Darla.

CHAPTER 33

Drew

"Sully, I need some help." My voice was raspy and weak.

After leaning against the window for an hour, my body had craved the drink I couldn't swallow earlier. Now I was hung over, exhausted, and heartbroken.

"What's up? You sound like shit."

"My girls are gone."

"Maybe it's for the best?"

"Shut it. I need someone to help me. She couldn't have gone far."

"I got a guy over near Miami. Russell. He's good. Does some work for me in my business when I need to investigate someone."

"Text me his number, okay?"

"Yes, sir. You need anything?"

"Just my kid and my woman."

"You still watching my money?"

"Your money's fine, Sull. Text me the number," I said, and I hung up.

The gym had already called. I was becoming a regular deadbeat. Missing workouts, drinking myself into a stupor, and not supporting my kid. Soon I'd be waking up on a park bench somewhere, stinking to high hell. I was like a homeless hobo without my family.

When my phone chimed with a text, I hit the number and called.

Russell was a University of Miami graduate who fell in love with the weather. His college girlfriend had gone missing after graduation, and he fell into this kind of work. Now, he found people and dug up dirt full time. I was sure his clientele was a who's who of Florida.

I told him what I knew. The sedan's make, model, and color. Red hair for Jules and strawberry blond for Darla, approximate heights and weights. Bryce's name and number, but I let him know I'd be visiting the ass myself as soon as we hung up.

Russell warned against doing that, and I politely told him to shut the fuck up.

I felt like such a chump. I didn't even know what bank she used or Darla's pediatrician. I was little to no help. Visiting Bryce was the least I could do.

"Come in," the dumbass called from behind his office door. When Bryce saw me, he stood up from behind his desk. "Shit. I didn't know it was you."

"Surprise." I mocked him with a smirk. "Have you heard from her?" I asked, cutting right to the chase. I had no need for small talk with the bastard.

"This morning. Still sick."

"You know that's bullshit."

"I also know Claire."

"You mean Jules. Obviously, not as well as you think."

"I know the more you push, the harder she pulls back. I've learned that over the years. I also know she's the biggest, baddest mama bear when it comes to Darla. You must've done something to scare her off."

"Don't fucking tell me what I did. You had her on the phone and didn't find out where the hell she was. You knew she was bullshitting."

"It's not my place to push her. I'm her friend."

"Some fucking friend. You're not even worried."

"I don't know what you want from me, Mr. King, but Claire . . . Jules . . .

is not my responsibility outside the restaurant."

"Fuck off." I turned to walk out the door, but remembered Russ. "Listen, some dude named Russell is gonna call you. I suggest you answer all his questions and be prepared to hand over your phone. Jules and Darla may not be your responsibility, but they sure as hell are mine."

I stormed out of the Southern and out to my car a desperate man.

Where the fuck was she?

Later that day, pacing my home office, I knew what I was about to do would turn out to be either incredibly stupid or naive. But I didn't care, because I was desperate.

I was used to being in control, and I could see that it wasn't helping me with Jules. She was gone, and shit was more out of control than if she were here.

I sat down in my desk chair and pulled up a window for Google to search for Jules's mom. It wasn't hard to find her, even though Smith was a common name.

How many Genevieve Smiths could there be in Ohio? Not many. In fact, there was only one, and when I found her number, I didn't hesitate to dial it.

"Hello?"

"Hi, Mrs. Smith, my name is Andrew King. I don't know if you remember me, but I was Juliette's coach at Hafton."

"I know exactly who you are, Mr. King, and I most definitely remember you. In fact, every time I see a new picture of my granddaughter, I think of you."

There you have it, folks. Jules's mother knows I slept with her.

"Um . . ."

"Did you know my daughter had a baby? I never understood why she didn't want to tell you. Please tell me she finally did."

"Yes, I know now. And I have to say, if I knew then, I would never have left."

I was trying to talk a good game. This woman was my only resource in trying to find Jules until Russ called.

"Well, she was a stubborn one, leaving Ohio the way she did. She thought I didn't know what was happening. She was always so naive. I guess not anymore with the whole single-mom thing."

"Do you know where she might be? She left town for a few days, and I'm trying to connect with her."

"Honey, I haven't kept track of her since she gave up a tennis scholarship for your damn baby."

Clearly, I wasn't going to get anywhere with this woman.

"What is it that you want, Andrew? I don't really understand."

"I want to do right by my daughter, and yours."

"Pretty sure that ship's sailed."

"All right, well, thanks. If you hear from her, can you tell her I called?"

"I won't," she said firmly, and the line went dead.

At least now I knew why Jules didn't have her mom helping her.

CHAPTER 34

Jules

"Mommy, tell me about when you were Jules," Darla whispered into the night.

We arrived in Jacksonville last night. I'd rented a room for cash at a motel near the water. Today we spent some time in the sand and eating junk food. I'd even fooled myself into thinking it was a mini-vacation.

"I loved tennis. Like you, sweetie. And I was a good student. Like you too."

We were snuggled in a king-sized bed, the TV glowing despite the volume being off.

"Tennis is fun." Darla curled in closer to me. "And turtles and fish. Maybe we'll see some dolphins in the ocean tomorrow?"

"Maybe in the morning. We have to go out early, because then we're going to head on to our next stop."

"Where?" Her tiny toes rubbed on my calf.

"It'll be a surprise for you, baby girl."

"I'm not a baby, Mom."

"You'll always be my baby."

"Will I go to a new school? I just made some friends, and we never did the sleepover."

This was something I didn't get. I never had close friends. My mom wasn't affectionate, and growing up, I couldn't help but be standoffish. No matter what anyone said, I blamed myself for what happened at my first school. If I had just tried a bit harder to be cool, fun, easygoing . . . anything other than myself.

"And I like Ms. Green and Drew."

"I know, honey."

Stupid Drew. He'd made me think I was normal back then, and not the odd duck out. He made me feel wanted.

Darla sneaked up on my cheek with a kiss. "But I love you the most."

At least I knew I hadn't repeated history. I gave her love and affection, unlike my mom. Although, I'd just taken her father away from her for the second time.

"You'll have friends no matter where you are, Dar. You're so lovable."

"I like my new ones. That's it, but yeah . . ." Her words drifted off, as faint as the light of the TV. Her breathing evened out and she relaxed, her weight sinking into my chest.

Most parents complained about sleeping with their kids. They took up too much room. They snored. They kicked. They needed their space.

Not me.

I fell asleep thinking of how much I loved my daughter, and how I at least did one thing right in life.

"Mom, Mom."

Someone shook my arm.

"Hmm?"

"Mom."

This time the shake was a little harder.

"Darla! You okay?" Instantly awake, I popped up in bed like I'd been struck by lightning.

"There's someone knocking on the door."

That's when I heard it. A few raps on the door, followed by a hand smacking the wooden surface.

"Go into the bathroom," I told Darla.

Once she was safely inside the bathroom with the door closed, I walked over and looked through the peephole. On the other side was a big guy, maybe six foot four, a golden beard covering the lower half of his face and a baseball cap pulled low over his eyes. Next to him was Drew, also sporting some scruff, wearing ripped jeans and a ratty polo shirt. He didn't look good.

"Jules, I know you're there," Drew called out. "I can see the shadow of your feet under the door. Open up."

I opened the door just a crack, but left the chain securely fastened. "Who the heck is the big guy?"

"Russ. He helped me find you."

"Is he a lawyer?"

"What?" Drew pressed his face near the crack, coming close enough to smell my breath.

I whispered, "A lawyer? Someone who's here to take Darla away?"

"Fuck no." He stepped away from the door and raised his hands in the air. "I'm not trying to take Darla away, Jules." His eyes were wide, and his words came out in short breaths. He seemed offended at my accusation.

"She's mine."

"Yes, I know. Ours. But I never want to take her mom away from her."

"Can we come in?" the big dude asked. "It's looking a little weird with us standing out here."

I unlatched the chain, and just as Drew walked inside, Darla opened the bathroom door.

"Drew!" She ran and jumped into his arms.

"Heya, superstar."

Held in Drew's arms, Darla stared down the big guy as if he were a short kindergartener. "Who are you?"

"I'm Russ, a friend of your parents."

My eyes glazed over at the word *parents*, and I felt faint.

"Jules!"

"Mom, I don't have parents . . ."

Those words echoing in the room were the last I heard before I actually did faint.

I came to on the bed, my feet up on a pillow, my head propped in Drew's lap. Darla sat next to me, dressed for the day and licking a lollipop.

"Ugh," I groaned.

"Mommy, are you okay? You fainted. Drew asked me if you ate yesterday, but I couldn't remember. Did you?"

"I did, baby girl." I tried to sit up, but Drew held me still.

"Take it easy."

"Mr. Russ knew my dad too, like Drew. A long time ago," she said.

Apparently Drew had fixed the situation, the crisis averted.

Of course.

He was the hero, and eventually I'd be the bad guy.

"Russ is going to drive my car, and I'm going to take you and Darla home after some breakfast."

"We need to get back for my tennis lesson tomorrow, Mom."

I closed my eyes, blocking out the sun and the sight of my girl, cooing after her father once again.

"It's time for us to go, Jules."

I nodded. Drew helped me up and walked me to the bathroom, where I did my thing and slipped on some clothes.

Thankfully, Russ was gone when I came out of the bathroom. Darla was now sitting next to Drew, telling him about the ocean.

"Turtles are my favorite, but fish too. And today, we were gonna look for dolphins. When I grow up, I'm gonna be a sea doctor. Isn't that awesome?"

"It sure is, superstar. What about your tennis?"

"Of course, I'm going to play tennis too. I'm going to do it all like Mom."

"That's right," he said, reaching over to smooth her hair out of her face. He looked at her with an adoration I wished I'd been on the receiving end of at least once in my lifetime.

Of course, Darla swatted his hand out of the way and shook her hair out, leaving it messy the way she liked it.

Come to think of it, thank God she liked messy, because her life was going to get all kinds of it.

Over pancakes and coffee and juice, Drew laughed with Darla and told her how glad he was she had this little trip.

Walking back to the car, he whispered to me, "Don't try a stunt like this again. I'm not taking Darla from you. I want to *share* our daughter. I mean it."

Unable to meet his eyes, I stared forward. "Drew . . ."

"Nod if you hear me, Jules, right now. We can talk later, but now let me know you understand me."

I didn't know if I understood, but I nodded.

CHAPTER 35

Jules

"Why'd you do it?"

"Because of this." I waved a hand to indicate the scenery. It was Sunday night, and we were settled back in our apartment after Sunday went just as Drew had orchestrated. Darla had played tennis earlier today like she'd wanted. Then she'd had her smoothie and bagel.

Her dream was coming true, and I was in a bad nightmare. There had been no other choice; Drew made it clear I needed to call Molly and take a break to talk with him.

"The beach? The ocean? The glass of wine in your hand?" Drew asked, his eyebrow lifted, his T-shirt blowing in the breeze. "You've got to give me a little more than waving your hand in front of you."

I shut my eyes and inhaled the salty air. Or was that my tears?

Drew's chair screeched as he scooted closer. He ran a finger under my eye and kissed the saltiness away, then took my drink and set it aside.

"Were you trying to hurt me? Punish me?"

The tears flowed more freely now. It didn't matter how hard I closed my eyes, they poured out.

"I don't know," I choked out.

"Shhh." Drew placed a small kiss on my forehead. He pulled me close, holding me by the back of the neck as he whispered in my ear. "You can tell me anything, Jules."

"I don't know if I wanted to punish you or me. Maybe both. It was so selfish." I sobbed into his shirt.

"Stop," he said, his own voice raw. "When I left, I thought it was for the best. I didn't know about you or Darla. Now we do. It's not fair to her or me if you run every time you get scared."

I looked up, putting on my bravest face. "I'm not scared."

"Like hell." He stared me down. "Say it. You were scared."

"How do you know?"

"Because I was scared once, and I ran away from the best thing that ever happened to me. But like I said, the stakes are higher this time."

"Being with you, it's so perfect. It feels so right."

"Because it is right." His lips touched mine for a chaste kiss. We sat knee to knee, facing each other in our deck chairs.

"It should've never been." I wanted to refute everything he said, change his mind, argue until I was blue in the face.

"Take a drink." He handed me my glass off the table. "Relax. It was and it is and it should've been, because we created a child."

"A child I kept from you."

"You can't keep punishing yourself. I left. I made the first mistake."

"Why are you the wise one here?"

"Because I'm so much older."

"Oh, please. I feel like I'm a million years old tonight. Worn out, tired."

"Because you are worn out. You've been doing everything on your own, but I'm here now. Thank God, because your mom certainly isn't rushing to help you."

"What in the heck are you talking about?"

"I may have called your mom."

"You what?" I wasn't sure I heard him correctly with the ocean roaring in the background.

"I called your mom, looking for you."

"Oh my God, what did she say?" The tears dried up and I felt a bubble of nervous laughter rising in my throat.

"She pretty much bitched me out."

"Your funeral calling her, but she does love Darla in her own way. She's the only person my mom's really loved since my dad."

"I'd suffer anything to have you back, Jules. You have to know that. You're all that I want."

"I'm sorry. I do, but can we put it behind us? I got spooked. My emotions were so amped up or something, and I went into crazy mother-hen mode."

"Next time you get into the mood, remember that I'm your rooster."

This time I laughed so hard, I gave the waves a run for their money.

The next morning, I gave Bryce some crap story about needing space from all the shit swirling around me. He bought my excuse, especially since I was back on the schedule and opting for more lunches, which meant more evenings with Darla.

And Drew.

The next few weeks passed in a blur.

Drew, the hot-blooded man and the doting father, usually joined us for tennis at the park, always sneaking in an ice cream cone for Darla and plenty of naughty glances my way. He even took Darla to Rocky Brook a few Saturdays on his own. Of course, she'd come home high on Drew and strawberry smoothies. Sunday mornings, I would grab a coffee and watch her beat the heck out of the boys in her lesson.

Every so often, Drew would glance up at me and wink. I wasn't sure if it was about me or Darla's prowess.

We'd also had a few dates. He'd been selective and careful about pushing me, but Halloween wasn't the only thing sneaking up on us. His patience and time were both running short.

Darla was mesmerized with flyers for a costume party at the club, and I wanted her to trick-or-treat around our building. I'd probably end up working anyway.

Then Drew said he'd back me up if we told her the truth. It was a built-in bargaining chip to get what he wanted.

Against my better judgment, he'd slept over two other times, but he kept pushing for a more full-time arrangement. I feared it was only a matter of time before he took the matter into his own hands.

I continued to hold tight to my excuse: Halloween was still three weeks away.

"Did you check in with Molly?" Drew asked as I made my way back from the ladies' room to our table at Prime Italian.

We'd driven to South Beach for the evening. It was a Friday night, and Molly was at my apartment with Darla. Drew wanted her to drive Darla over to his place to sleep, and then she could spend the day with him when I left for work.

My job was another sore subject, but tabled for the moment at Drew's insistence at our spending the night at his place.

"Darla's watching a movie and tired. I'm not going to have Molly move her for no reason."

"Making you two breakfast isn't a good enough reason?"

"Drew, come on. It's enough."

He poured more red wine into my glass. Our plates had already been cleared, and we were lingering at our corner table on the front patio. The meal probably cost more than my monthly rent.

"I want you there all the time, Jules. I've had enough of doing it this way. I want you in my bed, sleepy and droopy eyed when I get home from the gym. And I need my daughter in my house. It's my job to protect and take care of her."

"I want that too."

It was the first time the words had fallen from my mouth. They were quiet and hesitant, almost ashamed to make themselves known. I blamed the wine, but in reality, Drew had won. Just like I predicted would happen.

"So, let's do it. Let's tell Darla. She's smart, resilient. She'll be fine."

"What will this mean for her massive crush on you?"

"Only one girl for me. In that way."

I laughed; I couldn't help it. He knew what happened when he got silly

178

cheesy with me.

"I wonder what all the girls from the team at Hafton would say if they knew about us?"

"So, that's a yes. We're going to do this."

"I didn't say that."

"Say yes."

"To what?"

"To everything."

"Everything?" I asked.

"Yep."

"I don't even know what that means." I guzzled the last dregs of my wine.

"It means we become a real family, make it legal and all that."

"Nope. Not ready for that."

"It's your game, Jules. The ball's in your court. Every advantage is yours . . ."

"Stop! No more lines. Yes, I'll consider moving in after we tell Darla."

"When we get married, we should invite the old team to the wedding."

I almost spit out my wine. "No, just no."

"Why not? I wonder what happened with all of them."

"Who, Stacia?"

I couldn't help myself. Here I was sitting across from the man at a chic five-star South Beach restaurant, paparazzi and Ferraris lining the sidewalk, and while he begged me to move in with him, I was *jealous*. Insanely, stupidly jealous.

"Not Stacia. Only one tennis coed for me, Jules-y," he said and winked.

"Um, no Jules-y needed." I laughed like a giddy girl. This was fun. More fun than I'd had in years.

"Lulu and Hilary knew I was prego. They thought it was Lamar."

This got me the dirtiest of looks from Drew. If you googled *if looks could kill*, his snarl would come up.

"Who's jealous now, Drew-y?"

"Don't go there," he grumbled. "You're talking about my woman and my daughter, so there's no need to mention Lamar in the same breath. Yes, I was foolishly jealous of him back then. But you had my baby and you're back where you belong, so fuck him."

"Well, they knew. They swore they wouldn't tell, but we also pinkie-promised to stay in touch, and I didn't."

"Lord knows, no one could find Claire Smith. That's like looking for a musclehead on a motorcycle down here."

"Maybe they told someone when I never kept in touch, but they didn't know it was you. I don't even think they expected."

"It would be fun to see their faces if they found out. We're definitely inviting them to the wedding, Jules-y."

"One step at a time, Drew," I said with a scowl, but he was wearing me down.

"Go ahead. Text Molly and have them go back to my place so I can take my time later with you. That's my one step for tonight."

"Drew, listen." I set my glass down and looked into his eyes. "We have to do this my way. I'm not having Molly uproot Darla to your place. If you want to come back to my place, you can."

"I don't want Molly watching her tomorrow night. I want Darla with me. I'm sick of the food at the Southern, and I don't feel like watching you work. All those nasty guys and Bryce, and there's no reason for it."

I'm pretty sure I growled, "Enough."

"Okay, okay. But Darla's with me." Drew stood and helped me up. "Want to walk on the sand before we get back in the car?"

"Sure."

Once we took off our shoes, Drew held both pairs in his hand and took my fingers in his other. Our bare feet in the sand, we walked along the ocean's edge.

"I love your hair down like this." Drew stopped in his tracks and spun me toward him, never letting go of my hand.

"I'm such a rebel without my bun."

His laugh was warm like honey and deep like the Atlantic. It coated my soul, soothing my nerves.

"We should make another baby."

This time I laughed. "Drew, let's get through telling our first baby that you're my baby daddy."

"I know, but I want more kids."

"I can't right now, can't discuss it. Tell me what you're going to do with Darla tomorrow instead."

He squeezed my hand and started us moving again. "Tennis. Probably go to the club so we can eat afterward. Please don't laugh, but I also have these math workbooks . . ."

"What?"

"Yeah, I ordered them online because she's so smart. I know she likes Ms. Green, but I think she needs more. Numbers are my thing, so I thought I'd do a little extra."

It was like a fuse went off in my brain—like a short circuiting of all that was reasonable and right.

"I think I just fell in love with you all over again," came tumbling out of my mouth. I couldn't snatch my hand back fast enough, slapping it across my own lips.

"Oh yeah?" Drew turned to face me, and even in the moonlight, I could make out his cocked eyebrow mocking me.

"Yeah." My reply was so quiet, it was almost lost in the crashing waves.

"Well, I never stopped loving you, babe."

And just like that, we both burst into laughter. Only Drew knew how to break through the tension.

"Come on. Let's go back to your place and practice making another baby."

With me curled against his chest, the water lapping behind us, we made our way to his car.

Back at my apartment, Drew paid Molly like he'd been doing that sort of thing for years.

"Have fun, Claire . . . I mean, Jules," Molly said, adding a wink as he opened the door for her to leave.

Oh God, my sitter is thinking about me having sex. I turned to look for Drew, but he was MIA.

It didn't take me long to figure out where he was—a small sliver of light from the nearly closed door to Darla's room gave him a way. He found his way in there each and every time he came over.

I pushed the door open and there he was, sitting on the edge of Darla's bed, watching her sleep. His gaze didn't move from her chest rising and falling. His hand rested on her foot, and I saw his thumb running figure eights over the blanket.

A little wobbly with emotion, I made my way to him, pretending I wasn't having the urge to make another baby STAT. He sensed my nearness and brought his free arm around the back of my thighs, but never pulled his gaze from Darla.

It was in this tender moment of truth that I decided to make my family whole. It was time to set my wrongs right, no matter what it meant for me in the long run. There was no way Drew wasn't in it for forever with Darla.

He bent over and placed a kiss on her forehead, then stood and whispered, "Let's go to bed."

Inside my room, I became the aggressor. A puma born in a woman's body, I needed to claim my man. I shut the door quietly, turning the lock and pushing his back into the wood. Before he could put his mouth on my lips, I dropped to the floor, my knees hitting the carpet and my hand going for the zipper of his jeans.

My fingers grazed his abdomen, pushing his white Henley shirt up and exposing his tanned skin. With my index finger, I circled his navel and traced a path down his pleasure trail. Adding my thumb to the mix, I undid his button and drew his zipper down.

There he was on display in front of me—hard, reaching, ready, and commando.

When he sifted his fingers through my hair, I looked up at him.

"Jules, baby, you have no idea what this sight does to me."

I didn't answer, just opened my mouth and grasped his length in my hand, guiding it toward my lips. At first, I teased the tip and taunted his hardness, pumping up and down, barely able to reach my fingers all the way around his girth.

When he let out a low moan, I took all of him. This time, he released a growl, and that was all I needed to keep taking him deep. With long, languid movements, I brought him to climax. I think he warned me it was going to happen, but I was way too into the moment. I kept at it until he released down the back of my throat.

Before I could register anything but the sublime pleasure on his face, Drew hoisted me up and onto the bed, returning the favor before making love to me.

Twice.

CHAPTER 36

Drew

Jules was still asleep when I awoke a little before six. I slipped out of bed, checked on Darla, and left a note that I went to the gym. I snatched my gym bag from the trunk and was there as soon as they opened the doors.

Ignoring the blonde on my right, I beat the shit out of the elliptical. It was crazy . . . I'd slept only a handful of hours after having the best head ever and blowing my load twice, and yet I'd never felt younger.

It could have also been because I couldn't wait to get back. The faster and harder I worked out, the sooner I'd be with my girls.

"Hey, Drew," the girl at the desk called after me as I made my way to leave. "Where've you been?"

"With my daughter—and wife-to-be."

She had zero response.

In my car on the way back, I decided to put an addition on my house. I needed a home gym. I didn't like this bullshit of leaving in the morning anymore.

"Morning," Jules said in a hushed voice when I walked back into the apartment.

"Dar still asleep?"

She shook her head. "Watching something on TV in my bed."

"I knew you needed that new TV in there for something."

"It wasn't necessary."

"Well, you could've let me put it in her room like I wanted . . ."

"King, you can't just walk into her life and spoil her," she whispered over the rim of her mug.

"Why? She's my princess."

"Gah," Jules said, pretending to bang her forehead into the wall.

"Dar?" I called out when I was near the door.

"Drew, in here!"

"Get your bum out here. Your mom and I are taking you to Albert's."

"Woo-hoo!" Darla came stampeding out of the bedroom, wearing hot-pink pajama bottoms and a Rocky Brook T-shirt.

"Nice shirt. Let's go play later, yeah? I want to work on your serve."

"I don't like the serve. It gets boring."

"Gotta be able to serve, superstar, to beat the big boys."

"'Kay."

"Let's go, Jules. Put on some yoga pants and slap on your big-girl panties. Time to come clean."

She gave me the stink eye, and yeah, I knew I was being bossy.

Fuck it. I was too energized to care.

It took fifteen minutes for those two to reappear. Jules was freshly showered, her hair slicked back into a low ponytail, and wearing an oversized gray off-the-shoulder sweatshirt and leggings.

Darla, my wild child, was in floral leggings and an electric-purple T-shirt, her hair a holy mess all around her face.

"You look gorgeous, both of you. Let's go. I'm starving."

When we got outside, I lifted Darla on my shoulders.

"You're all sticky, Drew."

"I was too excited to change after the gym."

"Excited for what?"

"You'll know soon enough."

This set her off, and she demanded the whole way to Albert's, "Tell me!"

With a fresh coffee in front of her, Jules blew on Darla's hot cocoa and cut her bagel with cream cheese into quarters. Neither was necessary, but I assumed Jules needed to keep herself busy.

I nodded at Jules and took a sip of my coffee.

"Dar, Drew and I have something to tell you."

"I think I know!"

"Yeah?" I asked, setting my coffee down.

"You're my dad."

"Darla! What? What makes you say that? Who told you that?" Jules looked fifty shades of green. I almost felt bad for her, but I couldn't because I was getting my daughter.

"He is, right? I knew it!" At this, Darla got out of her seat and started jumping in place.

I couldn't have cared less where this all came from—to breathe in her excitement was better than oxygen—but Jules was glaring at me as if I were the one who had spilled the beans.

"Darla? Sit down and tell me where you learned this." Jules was curt, more so than I would have been, but I'd only been a parent for two months.

"Ms. Green. Mommy, she begged me not to say anything. She was nice about it."

"What do you mean? Begged?"

"She's so nice, and I said that Drew babysat me when I was sick. And she said, 'It's not babysitting when it's your dad.' I told her he wasn't my dad, and she said she was sorry. She explained that she thought we looked a lot alike, so she thought he was."

Jules closed her eyes and took a deep breath. Opening them again, she said, "You can't keep secrets from me, Darla."

"I know, but Ms. Green said it would hurt your feelings if I said anything."

"Still, no secrets." She bunched Darla's hands in hers, then brought them to her mouth and kissed away. "I love you too much for there to be secrets, but I'll forgive you this time because I kept a big one from you. Drew is your daddy."

At this, Darla pulled away and leaped into my lap, nearly knocking over her hot cocoa. "I got my birthday wish," she whispered to Jules, and kissed my cheek. "Plus, Danny at tennis said his mom said you look like my dad too."

"When?" This time it was me grumbling. Stupid Danny's mom had been trying to get in my pants for a year.

"When we were picking up the balls. I told him to shut it."

"Atta girl," I told my superstar.

Jules rolled her eyes and took a big gulp of her coffee.

She'd adjust to giving up some control.

Eventually.

CHAPTER 37

Jules

D arla was a question-asking machine, wanting to know *everything* about before she was born. It was a headache-inducing task to make the story as innocent and benign as possible, but I owed her the closest version to the truth as I could create.

Drew worked near Hafton.

I'd been taking a class or two.

We both loved tennis.

We met, fell in love, created a baby.

Then came the hard part . . . explaining Drew's absence.

"Blame me. Do what you need to, babe. This shouldn't be on you," he whispered in my ear as we headed up the walkway to his house. He had a surprise for Darla that couldn't wait.

I shook my head. I couldn't make Drew out to be the bad guy. He'd hurt me, but that didn't mean Darla deserved to grow up without a dad.

"Dar, Drew and I had a fight one day, and we were both stubborn. You know how I always say we shouldn't hold a grudge—you know what I mean, bad thoughts on someone? Well, I did. I held a grudge, and I did a stupid thing. I left Ohio with you in my belly, and I didn't tell anyone but Grandma G."

"Oh," she said. "So, you would've been with me?" she asked Drew.

"Of course, but you know what? God does funny things, and he didn't want me to meet you until you were this old, superstar."

"Yeah?"

She blinked back tears until Drew said, "Yep, I know it. Maybe so I could see how smart and funny you were going to be. And an amazing tennis player."

Once we were inside, Darla began running around Drew's museum of a house.

"Wait here a sec," he yelled from the kitchen, then walked toward what I thought was the laundry room.

Darla plopped down on the white leather sofa and bounced from one butt cheek to the other.

"Here you go, superstar." Drew handed Darla a new tennis racquet, top of the line, complete with hot-pink grip and string.

A smart man, he knew I was going to protest, so he cut me off by giving me a quick shake of his head, mouthing *no*.

After that, it was all fun and games and plans. Darla said *jump*, and Drew said *how high*.

"Mommy, Drew said we're moving here and I can pick a room . . . I mean, Daddy!"

I took a deep breath and let my new reality wash over me. Everything was about to change, and my daughter was taking it in stride way better than I was.

By the end of the day, I craved the mundane task of working despite Drew's private warning. "Not for much longer," he whispered to me as I left his place to go get ready.

"Drew . . ." I sighed.

"You can do anything or nothing."

"I can't do nothing."

"I know, babe. You're in the serving box, I swear."

But I knew he didn't really mean it when I got to work and Bryce called me into the office. "Tell me, Claire—I mean, Jules. Do you not have any respect for me? As a friend? Coworker? Boss?" His eyes were narrowed, dripping with animosity.

"What are you talking about?" I leaned against the doorjamb in my white shirt, black slacks, comfortable clogs, and purple tie, staying as far away as possible.

"Like I told you before, I was here for you when no one else was," he said smugly from behind his desk. "I told that cocksucker King the same. Where the hell's he been all these years?"

"I know you were, Bryce, but I'm not sure what I've done to get this treatment. I missed that one weekend, but otherwise I've been working a full schedule and taking lunches. Please leave Drew out of this," I said, trying to defuse the situation.

"I'm not talking about your schedule or work ethic," he said, slurring the last word or two.

As he stood from his desk and approached where I was standing in the doorway, I wondered if he was drunk. When he got close, breathing into my personal space, my suspicions were confirmed.

"Bryce, I think you should let me call you a cab to take you home. You're not acting like yourself, and you're going to regret it."

"No way. I'm talking about your boy toy calling over here and making demands. I'm acting like myself, and I for damn sure don't regret anything coming out of my mouth."

I considered going to get another server as backup, but didn't want to air my dirty laundry in front of the entire world. Today had been emotional enough.

"Your guy, he went on and on. Give you a small section, not to overwork you, blah, blah, more bullshit. And the icing on the cake? Keep an eye out for roving eyes when it comes to the mother of his child. Like I haven't been doing that for years."

"What are you going on about, Bryce? I've always taken care of myself." I took a step back, because even though my blood was boiling over Drew's little stunt, Bryce's proximity was making me more than nervous.

"He did say that. And let me ask you this again. Who kept an eye out when he wasn't around?"

I decided my pride would have to take a hit, and turned to run get help.

I didn't get far. Bryce took hold of my face, and I wish I could have called it a caress, but it wasn't.

"You're hurting me, Bryce," I forced out as his fingers squeezed my cheeks, drawing my mouth near his.

"Me. I kept an eye out," he gritted out, and then kissed me.

His kiss was bruising in a bad way. Rough, forced, not one bit tender, and tasted like tobacco and booze.

I said, "Stop," into his mouth, but he didn't. Finally, I stomped on his foot as hard as I could and wrested myself away.

"Shit," I muttered. My clog had done a number on his foot—Bryce was bent over in well-deserved pain—but my ankle had turned when I brought my foot down. Now I couldn't put weight on it.

"Claire, I'm sorry. It's just—"

"No just. I quit." I turned and limped to the back room and fell onto the bench.

Shit, shit, shit. My right foot was swelling out of my shoe. With my head in my hands, I felt the tears come. Bryce and the Southern had been my rock. Now that was destroyed.

Why hadn't I seen through Bryce's real feelings for me?

Because I had always been too clouded with memories of Drew. That's why.

Drew had no right, making demands of my boss, but neither did Bryce. I knew Drew's BS came from a good place, but still he shouldn't have done that . . . and now I couldn't drive. Hell, I could barely stand.

Who the hell was I supposed to call? Drew?

No way. I was too pissed. And he would go ballistic.

So I decided to text Molly.

On my way out, Bryce tried to stop me. "Wait, Claire," he hollered.

"It's Jules," I yelled back, limping to the back door.

"Wait! Please."

"No, and if you're smart, you won't drag Drew into this. That'll be a beat down and a lawsuit for you. Just send me my paycheck and stay out of my life. Go home and sober up, Bryce."

With that, I went outside. The fall night air only slightly cooled my temper. I leaned against the brick wall until the sight of Molly's headlights only lifted my spirits briefly.

CHAPTER 38

Drew

Best Saturday night ever.

I might as well have been a teenage girl riding an emotional high after her senior prom. That's how my chest continued to rise and fall—with pride, completion, devotion.

God, I was a sap.

No surprise, I'd let Darla stay up until ten. *When Mom's away, the kids will play.*

Now as I sank into my couch, I chuckled over my Scotch.

We'd spent an hour going through the house, discovering a few secret hiding places and deciding the guest room in the back would be hers. It was the larger of the two, and had a small balcony facing the ocean. I hoped Jules wouldn't argue it wasn't safe; I planned to have safety locks installed on the balcony doors.

Right now, the room only had a small couch and a TV in there, but I promised Darla we would go the very next day and get everything she needed.

She wanted to paint it silver with hot-pink stripes.

Of course, I'd agreed to that combo of paint colors. I made a mental note to text my contractor the next day as I focused on the floor-to-ceiling glass, staring at the ocean.

After our house tour, we'd gone to the club, hit two baskets of balls, and eaten dinner on the terrace. Grilled cheese for her and a cheeseburger for me; french fries, smoothies, and apple pie for us both. Like I said, it was the best Saturday night I'd had in a long time.

Maybe ever.

At home, we'd watched several episodes of an Animal Planet TV show I was sure Jules would kill me for letting her watch, but it was educational. I couldn't help that it included a baby whale being born.

This somehow led to one of Darla's favorite subjects. Turtles. We planned to get one the of those next day too.

When I tucked her in, kissing her forehead and both her cheeks, she said, "'Night, Daddy."

I nearly collapsed in the swell of emotions. It was a lot—even for a ballbuster like me.

"Love you, superstar," I'd answered.

At eleven, I took my second Scotch upstairs and checked on her. She was fast asleep. I stood in the doorway admiring her for several beats until I heard a car door open and close outside.

Good. That Bryce prick listened to me and sent Jules home early.

Which was why I wasn't at all prepared for what I saw outside the front door. Molly was helping Jules up the stairs, who had a boot on her foot and crutches in one hand. Her free hand held on to Molly, her right foot lifted in the air.

"What the ever-loving fuck?" I ran down the stairs. "Jules, stop."

"Drew, not now."

"Here." I shoved my Scotch at Molly and lifted Jules into my arms. "Take these too," I said, nodding at the crutches.

"It's not her fault, Drew," Jules argued as I carried her up the stairs.

"What the hell happened? What the fuck is Molly doing here?" The questions vomited out of me as anger seeped out from my pores.

"I got hurt. I called her. Period."

"No shit. Why the fuck didn't you call me?" I asked, shoving the door open with my hip.

"Put me down. This isn't good for your knee."

"Shut up, Jules." I laid her down on the sofa. "Molly? Want to enlighten me?"

"Hey." She put her hands up in mock surrender. "I didn't do it."

"Molly, thanks," Jules said from the couch, her arm flung over her face. "Go home. I owe you big-time. I'll call you in the morning."

Then I saw something red on her face, a fingerprint, and I fucking lost it.

"What the hell is that?" I dropped to the floor and moved Jules's hand.

"I'm going to explain, but you need to promise to remain calm. Remember, Darla is here."

At the mention of my daughter's name, my anger faded a little. I took a deep breath and nodded. "Please, Jules. I'm dying here. What happened? You have a mark on your face and a broken foot."

She proceeded to tell me about an argument with Bryce over my call, explaining that he then got handsy with her, forcing his lips on her.

"Take a drink," she insisted at the mention of his mouth touching hers. "He was drunk and out of line, but you shouldn't have called him. Still, he was out of control, and I . . ."

My head swam with rage and thoughts of revenge. I think she said something about smashing his foot, but she'd broken hers in the process. And twisted her ankle.

"Why the hell didn't you call me?" I ran my hand up her boot.

"Because I was mad. I am mad. You can't bulldoze my affairs, butt in where you don't belong. I don't need your protection. Lucky for you, I'm disgusted with Bryce right now, and yes, I quit my job. But I'm going to get another, and you can't bully every one of my bosses. I've been independent for a long time."

"Did you see a doctor? A real doctor? Not an intern or resident?" I couldn't listen to that other crap right now. Later, I would promise to stay out of her shit. Not now.

"Did you hear me?"

"Yeah, but tell me about your foot. I can't discuss you working right now. You're injured." I stood up and paced the room like a caged animal. "Did you press charges? He touched you . . . I'm going to beat the fuck out of him. You know that?"

"No, you're not. You're going to leave him alone. And no, I'm not pressing charges because I just want to be done with him and that place, okay? Listen, we're making a new life. We have to be on the same page."

"I know, but . . . no, it's not okay. I am going to deal with that prick, but we can finish this discussion in the morning. Let's get you out of those clothes and into bed."

I couldn't listen to her bullshit anymore. I would take matters into my own hands whether Jules liked it or not.

She started to stand, and I went to lift her. "No, my crutches, please."

"Ugh, you're going to be a stubborn one with this."

"Drew, let me be."

She held on to the banister and hoisted herself upstairs, and stood outside the guest room. I cracked the door open for her, and she leaned against the jamb and peeked in on our daughter.

"Did you have a good night?"

"The best." I kissed behind her ear, pulling her hair away.

"She looks happy, even in her sleep."

"She'll be happier now that she has more time with you."

That got me an eye roll before she hobbled down the hall on her crutches to the master bedroom.

Sitting on the edge of the bed, Jules rolled her shoulders and took off her solo clog. I came close and lifted her shirt above her head, taking my time, inhaling her hair and holding her close.

"I need a shower. Do you think you could hold me up in there on one foot?"

"I thought you would never ask."

"Not now, Drew. Not now. I'm exhausted, and I want to get to bed."

"Just lean on me, babe. Tonight, tomorrow, forever. That's all I want."

CHAPTER 39

Jules

sat up in the bed made for a king, leaning back into a mountain of pillows—big ones, little ones, satin ones, patchwork ones—and put my foot up on a huge stack at the foot of the bed meant for that exact purpose.

I watched Drew walking back into his—*our*—room.

Within two days of my foot being broken, he'd had a gang of twelve packing, moving, and unpacking our stuff. There wasn't much, so I didn't think that many people were necessary, but they also assembled Darla's new furniture and painted her room.

Silver and pink, exactly like she wanted.

Oh, and then there was the mounting of a turtle habitat near the balcony door.

Mikey Oliver, our new turtle, lived in there. Yes, that was his full name. Calliope Kitty, our new cat, made herself comfortable wherever she saw fit. At the moment, she was burrowed next to the pillow where my foot rested.

Within two weeks, Drew's bachelor pad had turned into a family home/petting zoo. There was talk of a rural house in the Midwest and a pony. I couldn't even think about it.

Basically, Drew was a yes machine when it came to Darla, and since I was currently a helpless gimp, I allowed my daughter to become the most spoiled little girl on the planet, giving Drew carte blanche to undo everything I'd done.

My pride was only slightly bruised. After all, I'd denied her this exact thing for the first six years of her life, so it wasn't my place to keep it from her anymore.

I owed her this—*him*. She deserved Drew and all that he could provide, mostly the love and adoration he gave easily and without measure.

Drew sat down next to me. "Hey."

His hair was a little longer and falling forward on his face. I couldn't help myself; I reached up and ran my hand through it.

"This is for you." He handed me a glass of wine.

"How's Dar? Did she want me to hobble in there? Say good night?" I started to push up from my resting place, wineglass in hand. It wasn't pretty.

"Whoa, hold your horses, Italian stallion. She was out before I finished the chapter, and no. She said to give you this." He kissed me on the cheek, letting his lips linger a bit longer, prickling my skin and making my heart beat faster.

"I guess I've officially been ousted between you and the foot. Did you just use a *Rocky* reference? Because I could beat you over the head with my crutch."

"You're beautiful like his wife, but tough like Rocky. That's my Hurricane Jules."

I rolled my eyes and sipped my wine. "You don't have to seduce me anymore. You've got me all locked up in your castle, and our daughter is so smitten with you, she's forgotten all about me."

"Nah, I'm just the bright new shiny object, babe. You're her whole world. She's always telling me *Mommy this* and *Mommy says that.* You brought her into this world; you'll always be number one."

"Tell that to her when she gets her first period."

"Shhh, I can't even think about that shit right now. God, no boyfriends, by the way. None."

I took another sip of my wine and let it course through my system, calming my frazzled nerves. Drew's mom was coming to visit soon, and Darla's teacher kept asking when we were getting married.

Between all of that and not working, my emotions were fried. I needed something more, but I wasn't sure what.

"Hey, you're zoning out. What's that smile for?" Drew asked me while running his hand up and down my thigh.

"I was just thinking how bored I was, but also how lucky I am because I have the luxury of picking what I want to do with my life now." Tears pricked at the back of my eyes.

"I wish you'd been able to do that from day one. I hate that you had to do what you did for so long, but the result was outstanding. Look what a fabulous young girl you raised. Our daughter."

"I hope that one day she gets to do whatever she wants."

His hand stilled on my leg, and he said, "Take a drink."

So I did. He seemed pretty determined and bossy.

"What was that . . . take a drink . . . all about?"

"We were drinking to Darla doing whatever she wants. I know she will. I can see it in her eyes. Her determination."

"Thank you," I whispered. I didn't want my life for my daughter. I wanted better, and somehow Drew inherently knew this.

"Also this. I got you something."

He slipped his hand into the pocket of his shorts and pulled out a shiny bauble. When he straightened it out, a very large *J* hung from a sparkling chain.

"Lean forward," he said softly.

He slid his hands around my neck and placed a diamond *J* on my chest. Of course, the chain sparkled because it was studded with black and white diamonds in tiny bezels.

"This is too much. What do I need this for? All I'm doing is lying in bed."

"Be quiet, Jules, and let me look at how beautiful you are."

"I love you, King."

"I know. Now, drink your wine and relax and hush."

"If I relax any more, I'll turn into a veal."

"You're a vegetarian. You can't."

We both laughed until Drew leaned in and kissed me, sweeping his tongue through my mouth.

"Actually, why don't we put the wine down . . ." He took the glass from me and set it on the night table, and leaned back again and covered my mouth with his. "You taste good. Bet you taste even better somewhere else."

His mouth traveled down my neck, pushing the *J* aside, skimming at the neckline of my sheer long-sleeved tee. He traced the trim with his tongue until a moan erupted from his chest. The tip of his tongue caressed my skin, starting a fever prickling below the surface.

"Stay right there." He popped up and went to lock the door.

"I can't exactly go anywhere."

"I kind of like it. You stuck in our bed."

He slipped out of his workout shorts and tossed his tee on the floor, then walked back toward me. At the end of the bed, he stood there in all his glory, naked and lean. Tattoos and tanned skin, more crinkles around his eyes and smoother hands than when we first met, and I never loved anyone so hard. Leaning down, he divested me of the big freaking boot and carefully removed my lounge pants.

"Leave it off," I said about the boot.

"Don't squirm then." He winked.

Climbing up beside me, he peppered kisses on my ear, sucked on the lobe and down my clavicle, then pulled off my shirt and slid his mouth along my side cleavage.

His breath hummed over my bra until he shoved the straps down and took my nipple in his mouth. Nipping and sucking, he took his time, my bra still shoved down.

"Jules," he moaned breathlessly.

"Please," I said in return.

He slid down my body until his mouth covered my hot spot, no longer nipping but taking his time. Lavishly. That's what I would call it.

Lavishly devoting himself to me.

It didn't take long for me to come undone. A fine sheen of sweat broke out on my brow, caused by the pulsing between my legs and trying to keep my foot still.

"I want you."

"You need to let me do all the work. You know the routine."

"I can't help it if my hips move." I smiled before he kissed me, tasting like me. It felt like more than love.

With his hand, he guided himself into me, one thrust, long and leisurely. He pulled back out, taking his time, and dived back in. That's what he did until I couldn't take it anymore, and let my hips come up and meet his thrusts.

"Jules . . ." This time he growled my name.

"It feels good. Let me."

And he did, driving into me as I met each thrust until we were both spent and satisfied.

"You going to marry me, Jules?"

We lay there, my head on his chest and his lips pressing soft kisses to the top of my head.

"What am I going to do with you, King Drew?"

"Now who's the corny one? Marry me. Don't make me beg." His hand caressed my side, his finger lingering on my breast, circling my sensitive area. Rinse and repeat.

"We're together. That's what matters."

"I want to get married soon, Jules. Soon. Don't forget."

"Why?"

"Because you're my everything. And why the hell not? I don't want to get corny or crazy romantic; I know that bugs you. But I want you to know you're mine."

"Now, you shhh. You're going to piss me off."

"Bet I can really piss you off . . ."

"What?" I squeezed my eyes shut but smiled.

"I bought Darla a *D* necklace."

"No, you didn't."

"She's already wearing it, so we can't return it."

"Tell me it wasn't diamonds."

"It wasn't."

I closed my eyes again, this time drifting off.

"It has yellow diamonds for my tennis superstar."

I pretended to be asleep.

The following night wasn't any better when it came to Drew making it known what he wanted. We went out for Italian with Sully and Rosie, and they insisted we bring Darla. Their kids were too busy for them, and Darla flirted like a pro with Sully.

"Uncle Sull, can you tell me again about your boat? Are we going to go on it soon? Will we see dolphins?"

"I can't believe I let her call him Uncle Sull after what he did to me the first time I met him," I said to Rosie.

"We didn't meet then," Sully said, and when I eyed him up, he changed his story. "Okay, I was acting like an arrogant jerk. It was men's night out. Blame the cigars and the whiskey."

"Sullivan, one more bad report about you and I'm leaving you for a tennis pro. Like Drew, young, virile, muscular," Rose interjected.

I blushed. Drew was certainly virile.

"He's not a pro," Sully argued, his manhood under attack.

"He's my teacher, Uncle Sull. That makes him a pro."

"And he was your mom's—"

"Sull, no need to go there," Drew said quickly.

We figured when the time was right we would tell Darla the truth about how we met, and where and when she was conceived. More importantly, someday she deserved to know why her dad wasn't in her life for the first six years.

"Speaking of calling you Uncle Sull," Drew piped up. "We should make it official, don't you think?"

"What do you mean, Daddy?"

I took a swig of wine and glanced at my foot in the boot stretched out to the side.

"Well, it's like in tennis when it's tied. Forty all. Your mom and I are at deuce, ad in. My ad. I have you, so that's my advantage, but I want her too. Then I win."

If smoke could have poured out of my ears and eyes, it would have.

"Dar, Dad wants to make it official. We have you and we live together, and that's enough. Whether we're married or not doesn't make us love you or each other any less."

"What's the hang-up?" Sully asked. *Freaking Sully.* "And yes, Darla, we'll see lots of stuff on my boat, and even fish."

"No, no fishing. I don't eat fish. Mom wants me to, but I said no."

The conversation was giving me whiplash, but this was my life now. Loving Drew, curious Darla, boisterous Sully, and caring Rosie. A crazy crew, for sure, but the first family and friends I'd had in a long time.

However, now I wished I could kick Drew under the table with my boot.

I didn't really know what my hang-up was. I suspected it was my mom and her unhealthy attachment to my dad. She was so obsessed with him and his ghost that she could hardly find it in her heart to love me. I guessed she did on her own terms, but still . . . marriage seemed unnecessary at this point.

"No hang-up," I explained. "Just not needed. And you know Drew always has to get what he wants, but this time, he's not."

"We'll see about that," my man countered.

Problem was, I was pretty certain we would.

"I want to get married," Darla added. "To Dad."

It's like they were playing doubles and I was still playing singles.

Ad out.

CHAPTER 40

Drew

Five weeks had passed since Jules broke her foot, and she was allowing me to take her to her final X-ray appointment. I was fucking grateful.

It had been a long few weeks—thirty-five days that didn't involve me beating the shit out of Bryce—but I got Jules and Darla instead. She drove a hard bargain, that woman. In exchange for my promise to leave the situation up to her, she agreed to move in right away.

I was a reasonable man, but this deal was as painful as getting a prostate exam. There wasn't a day I didn't want to call Russ and set something up to "take care" of Bryce. But Sully kept me on the straight and narrow. Mostly because Rosie fell in love with Jules, and threatened him to make sure I behaved.

"Excited to dump the boot?" I asked Jules as I drove her to her appointment.

"Yes, and then you can call off those caterers for Thanksgiving."

"No can do, babe. I already paid."

I hadn't, but fuck it. She wasn't going to stand there cooking all day for our mothers.

"But your mom—"

"My mom hasn't had a home-cooked meal in decades, and your mom doesn't deserve you going all out. We're doing it for Darla. End of discussion."

"I'm making dinner the night before, and dessert for Thanksgiving Day."

"Only if I can eat it off your naked body after Darla goes to sleep." This got me a big smile.

"Not to ruin the good mood, but you should know he's gone. I spoke to the other manager at the Southern, and Bryce left town. Took a job with a new Italian franchise in Orlando."

"Not far enough."

"Well, he's gone and my foot is healed, and we're living with you. What else do you want?"

"You to marry me."

"I walked right into that, didn't I?"

"I'd say more like hobbled."

She just shook her head and smiled while facing the window, thinking I couldn't see.

"You're going to give in eventually," I said while helping her out of the car with her crutches.

"Why? We already have a child and live together. If we get married, the girls from years ago . . . may find out."

"So the fuck what."

"Let's just go to my appointment, okay?"

Another week had passed and Jules was gearing up for both of our moms to come visit. Her mom hadn't seen Darla in at least two years, and my mom didn't even know she had a grandchild until a month ago.

To say Jules was tense would be the understatement of the year. The only time I'd seen her take a deep breath was when I said, "My mom is staying at the Boca Beach Club. This isn't fancy enough for her, plus she needs maid service."

Mom was single at the moment, and I was certain she'd be spending her free time searching for husband number four.

Other than hanging with Darla, Jules had holed up in the kitchen, cooking and baking and cooking some more. Apparently, making a mess provided her some sort of tension relief.

"I'm home," I called as I walked into the house after I slipped out of work around three.

"Hey," Jules said, out of breath and breathtaking in the kitchen. She wore tight-as-hell yoga pants and a long tank, an apron tied tight at the waist, and her hair up in her famous messy bun.

"Dar home yet?"

"She's going to Sydney's house today to play and have dinner, remember? She was going to go tomorrow, but you scheduled a tennis lesson."

"Right." Truthfully, I wanted Darla home all the time. Fuck playdates. Better she be with me, but Jules said it was important.

And now I was thinking she was on to something, because she was looking sexy as fuck in our kitchen and we had hours to ourselves.

"Here, taste this." Jules shoved a bite of muffin in my mouth.

I literally moaned. "This is good, better than good. What is it?"

"Zucchini and chocolate with a caramel ribbon."

"Babe, you're making food porn in here. Hope you're not trying to make me fat."

"Stop. Between you and your elliptical, you'll never be fat. Plus, I love cooking, being at peace in the kitchen. It's quiet and settling, so you'll have to deal with the calories."

"Give me some more," I demanded, and she did.

"You know, last Friday I brought some of those carrot cookies with the cream cheese icing when I picked up Dar from her playdate? The mom went wild for them. She asked what else I do, and I told her I cook and bake all vegetarian."

"Yeah?" I grabbed the spoon from the bowl and licked it.

"Drew, don't."

"Don't tell me don't. Tell me about the cookies."

"She asked me if I would cater a dinner for her. A vegetarian Mexican night, complete with desserts. Queso and quesadillas with grilled vegetables and dips, and a few bean dishes. I got so excited over the prospect of it.

Apparently, there are so many vegetarians and vegans down here, it's not PC to serve meat." Jules was so excited, she was practically dancing in place.

"Really?"

"I think I'm going to do it. If it goes well, I could start a vegetarian catering company. I could do that; I know food service. It's all I know."

"Babe, I like the way it sounds. You know a hell of a lot more than food service, but you definitely need a commercial kitchen. When you cook at home like this, I get all kinds of dirty thoughts. And I don't think that's good for business."

"Well, this woman asked me to cook in her kitchen, which is great, but yeah, I need a space. I'd have to take a loan from you, but my goal would be to pay you back."

I shouldn't be mad, because the fact she even considered taking a loan from me was progress. Still, it bugged me.

"Jules, it's not a loan. It's ours, and I say go for it."

"But I want to, and the cool thing is if I get big, then I could hire some staff, treat them right. I'd want to take care of people. Women. Single moms."

"No buts, and that's beautiful. I don't doubt you'll get big." Then I shut her up real quick with my tongue in my mouth and my hand on her ass. "But you're never paying me back," I mumbled into her mouth.

She didn't have time to respond because I gripped her from behind and slid her onto the white quartz counter. Good thing it was a mess, because we were going to make it messier.

Jules's hands went up the back of my T-shirt as I fumbled with her apron. I untied the flimsy piece of fabric and tossed it aside. Breaking free from her lips, I pulled my shirt overhead and yanked Jules's leggings over her bare feet, then her thong. After shoving her tank and bra to the side, I found her nipple and sucked until she squirmed.

I traced a finger over her top until it came to the top of her landing strip. When I spent a minute too long teasing her nub, she moaned, "Please," so I slipped in one finger, and then two. Her sticky fingers traced my waist.

"Love this," she whispered, and ran a fingernail around the outline of my newest tattoo.

A turtle, as requested by my daughter.

It wasn't nearly as badass as my scorpion, but it meant everything. The tortoise was slow, like our love. Jules and I were a slow-burning torch, one that never would fully extinguish. Of course, on the turtle's shell was the name Darla, because she was our protector in all of this, the hard casing that kept us together.

At some point, I couldn't think about the turtle anymore because Jules was riding my fingers and getting herself there, and I wanted to be a more active participant. Dropping to my knees—fuck the bad one—I put my mouth on her. It was my favorite meal.

It didn't take long for me to get her off. She came apart with a delicious moan, my name rolling off her tongue in that way that always made me hard. Afterward, I stayed the course, riding out her waves until Jules tugged on my hair.

Yep, it was long enough to do that now. I'd let it grow back out.

She yanked me up and sealed her mouth over mine, not one bit bashful about her taste all over my face and lips. Her delicate fingers tugged at my zipper and pushed my jeans over my ass. Lucky for her, I was commando. As usual.

"You can't walk around here with no boxers . . . I keep telling you," she grumbled. But I knew she liked it.

"I'm usually wearing pants."

Her hand wrapped as much as it could around me and started working me hard.

Fuck it, I couldn't wait. I pushed her back onto the counter, bowls flying and spoons landing next to her face, and shoved inside. I took a moment after I was fully seated to revel in my life. It was *love all*, or whatever you wanted to call it. Cat's game, a tie. Jules and I had both won. We had each other and our daughter.

And this—me deep inside her, no barriers except that she was on the pill. I had to convince her to marry me first, then babies.

One thing at a time, I reminded myself. It was like she was the teacher, and I was the student. She taught me well, so I had to go with her cues.

"Come on, King Drew."

She nudged my ass with her foot, and I started moving. I took her in long, leisurely strokes, my movements slow and seductive, until neither of us could take it anymore. Then I took her hard and fast, my thumb strumming her spot and the heel of her foot kneading my ass until we both exploded in climax.

"Babe, I don't think you're going to be able to cater anything out of this kitchen. Ever. Seeing you in that apron does something to me, and we're violating every health code in the book."

CHAPTER 41

Jules

Dinner was ready. I paced the kitchen while Drew went to the airport to pick up his mother. Luckily, my mom was being civil to both Drew and me—not loving, but tolerant—and was reading to Darla in the other room. Knowing Darla, she was probably reading to my mom. She wasn't one to sit around and listen to someone else. She was a take-charge person like her dad.

It was the night before Thanksgiving, and I'd made beef Wellington and eggplant parmesan. No way was I serving Drew's hot-blooded Southern mom only vegetables. I'd perfected my puff pastry the week before, and tried not to breathe while stuffing the slab of raw meat inside it.

The house smelled delicious, thanks to the apple-spice candles burning in the living room and the fruit cobbler in the oven. I smoothed my sweater and rolled my sore foot a little. It still ached from too much use, but hey, I needed to be mobile in order to cook.

"Mom!" Darla came running into the kitchen. "They're here."

I silently prayed she wasn't getting her hopes up over nothing.

"Why don't I fill the water glasses," my mom called, mostly wanting to avoid the introductions, I was sure.

I went to open the front door and saw Drew walking a step behind his mom, who had a huge bouffant head of blond hair and a face pulled so tight, her hairline was in the middle of her head. Biting the inside of my cheek, I kept myself from laughing. She was exactly as he'd described her.

She held her hand out to me. "Sharlene King Hagman."

Every finger was heavy with jewels; her wrist must have weighed more than Darla. Rows and rows of diamond tennis bracelets adorned her arm, interspersed with heavy bangles. I wasn't sure how she lugged it all around.

"Jules Smith."

"Soon to be King," Drew added.

"No rush," his mother said under her breath, then looked down at her granddaughter. "You must be Darla. You look just like your daddy, lucky girl."

Thankfully, Darla kept quiet. Even she was unsure of what to make of that remark.

"I'm Grandma Shar," Sharlene said, bending down.

"Nice to meet you," Darla finally responded, standing on her tiptoes to give Sharlene a kiss on the cheek.

"Don't you think this place is all wrong for a family, Drew?" She lifted her big sunglasses on top of her head as we made our way into the foyer. "All white and sharp edges. It's much more suiting to a bachelor. You probably miss that life. Not to mention, there's stuff everywhere. Ooh." She jumped to the side as Calliope brushed past her leg. "What in the heck?"

"That's Calliope, my kitty, and I also have a turtle. Want to see?"

"Perhaps later. This place is like walking onto a live set of a children's program."

"I love this house," Darla said, jumping from foot to foot. "Did you know we have an elevator in the back now? They're still building it, but it's going to connect the new room with the middle of the house and then the patio."

"How lovely. Expanding the brood, are we?" Sharlene eyed my flat stomach.

"No, Mom. I added on a third-floor gym. I didn't like leaving every morning to go to the gym, and then I miss Dar leaving for school."

"Oh. I never minded not seeing you in the morning. Then again, I needed

211

my beauty sleep."

She just kept steamrolling through the house, nitpicking. We needed a yard if we were going to be real parents, or maybe Darla would go to boarding school. "I'm a fan," she said.

Sharlene clearly had no patience for the lesser folk, which definitely included my mom and me. When meeting my mom, she barely muttered, "Hello there," looking down on my Midwestern mama, who wouldn't win any mother-of-the-year awards. But still, she was mine.

That's pretty much how the evening went. Sharlene picked on me, a little bit on Drew, ignored my mom, and treated Darla like a doll.

"Oh, look. She's so precious with her food all cut up. Who will do that for her at school?"

"Mom, we're not sending Darla to school. She goes to school here, and maybe next year, she'll go to private school."

That remark earned him a dirty look from me. He'd been on me about that, and I disagreed.

"Sharlene, what will you be doing while you're here?" my mom asked, trying to break the ice. I was pretty sure she felt bad for Darla.

"Oh, well, the spa is lovely, and I was hoping Drew would come and make use of the tennis facilities."

Drew piped up. "Darla plays. I'll bring her over." Darla, of course, loved this idea. "And you too, Jules. Time to try on that foot again."

"Don't force her." This came from Sharlene.

"You know what? This is my family, Mom. Jules is not going anywhere, and neither is Darla. Not school, nowhere. So, shut it."

After that, Sharlene was mostly curt, politely saying *no thank you* to dessert. The minute dinner was over, she asked Drew to take her back to the hotel.

Tomorrow was surely going to be an interesting Thanksgiving. With a caterer.

I was already dreading Christmas.

Jesus, I was trying to be a caterer and Drew hired someone else. I vowed to myself the holidays would never be like this again. Next year, I'd ask Drew to cough up some money and we would go away. It was worth it.

At the end of the weekend, we flopped on top of the bedcovers and lay tangled together, Drew's fingers running up and down my arm.

"It wasn't so bad," I whispered, lying.

"Jules, don't bullshit me." He pinched my skin, teasing me, taunting me.

"It was bad. Your mom basically hates me, and my mom . . . at least she loves Darla."

"My mom wants her to go far, far away."

"Like to the moon." I laughed out loud.

"Darla can stay under this roof until she's forty, for all I care." Drew pulled me up so we were face-to-face.

"Somehow, I don't think she'll like that plan."

"I like it. A lot." He ran his nose along mine. "A whole lot. That's my girl."

"Right now, I like you," I mumbled, pressing my lips to his.

"You do now?"

He kissed me with the passion of three men, our tongues meeting and twisting, like our legs. I felt my heat rub against his thigh, and I moaned.

"Touch me." I was desperate, hot and bothered for King, the man of my dreams. "Pinch me again."

"What?" He pulled back and looked at me, his brow furrowed, his eyes questioning me.

"I have to know this is real."

"It's real, babe. You, me, Darla, the fairy tale."

"I can't believe it. I just can't."

He kissed me again, stronger than before, headier than earlier. I didn't need any words. I believed.

I shoved down Drew's shorts, giving myself easy access to his commando ass. I nudged him closer so his hardness ran along my wetness. My panties were soaked, and he didn't waste any time tugging off my oversized T-shirt. His mouth latched onto my nipple, sucking hard and eliciting a long moan from me.

Next came my panties, tossed to the floor, and he was in me. My back to the mattress, his frame hovering over me, taking his damn sweet time moving in and out of me.

I thought about telling him my secret, but I didn't. I decided to enjoy this moment, revel in my belief and my man. There was no way he'd be mad about my little lie of omission. It wasn't exactly like keeping Darla from him for years. He'd be thrilled to learn I'd stopped taking the pill two weeks before, and I was waiting for just the right time to admit it.

Drew moaned my name in my ear and whispered, "Love you, babe. Since the moment I sat at your kitchen table, in awe of how strong you were."

At that moment, I decided to wait. He didn't need to know until I could tell him even better news.

EPILOGUE

Drew

"Daddy, look!" Darla's hand stretched to the left of the kayak, almost tipping her slim body into the Pacific.

"Whoa," I said, slowing my oar. "I see it, superstar."

"Look at it!"

A giant turtle swam just below the surface, and a school of fish darted about a bit deeper.

"Let's get out!" She tried to stand up in the kayak.

"One sec. Let's drop the anchor." I grabbed the weight from behind me and tossed it into the ocean, ensuring the kayak would remain nearby.

In our tiny wake, the fish and turtle moved quickly along the ocean floor, disappearing from view.

"Aw . . ."

"They'll be back, and there'll be more, baby girl."

"Yay! Can we go in the water?"

"First, we need our flippers."

Carefully, Darla slipped her feet into small flippers and I shoved mine into larger ones, making sure we didn't fall out of the kayak in the process.

"Okay, now your snorkel and goggles."

"Ouch," she said sliding the apparatus over her face. Loose hairs stuck to her cheek and wound their way in front of her goggles.

"I gotta say, you should've let Mom put your hair back in a neat bun."

"I'm fine. Let's go!"

"Ready, Freddy?"

"Ready, Heddy!"

"Go ahead."

I held her hand while she tossed her legs over the side and flopped into the water. The Hawaiian sun reflected off her bright yellow swim shirt.

"Come on," my daughter said, beckoning me.

She didn't have to ask twice.

I slid into the water and kicked until I was next to Darla. We floated for a minute, and then she took my hand and we swam around a bit. With our faces pressed into the water, the ocean came to life. Schools of fish, octopus, and turtles streaked by, the reason we were out kayaking in the Pacific.

Her small hand tugged on mine, and I turned to see her free hand point to the right. An entire turtle family swam right in front of us.

Sending Darla to private school had been the right choice, even though Jules fought me on it. Darla was incredibly smart, especially in the sciences. She loved sea life, and the teachers took care to make sure she had her fill at school. It wasn't a boarding school. My girl still spent every night at home.

Her school also happened to house Florida's top tennis program.

I rose to the surface, treading water as I watched Darla swim around, confirming what I already knew. There was no reason for my daughter not to have every advantage.

Of course, Hawaii had been her idea for our honeymoon after Jules agreed to do the deed. We'd gone to the justice of the peace at the city-county building one December afternoon when Darla finished school. My mom had proven to have zero interest in me, and Darla's mom was her mom. She picked what she wanted to get involved with. This wasn't high on her list.

After a quick civil ceremony, Sully and Rosie had taken us to Abba to celebrate. Over dinner where I first recaptured Jules, Rosie had asked if we were going on a honeymoon, and Darla piped right up.

"We should go to Hawaii."

Jules gave me a look that said *I know there's no way you're not taking her with us now.*

I'd missed six years of her life. Of course I said yes.

We planned it the next day, and here we were. Christmas in Hawaii with my girls.

"You tired? Want to paddle back to shore and get a smoothie?" I asked Darla when she popped back above water. "We can come back out tomorrow morning."

"We should bring Mom."

"Want to know a little secret?" I dragged her near, holding her wet body up and close to my face. I kissed her nose and whispered, "I kind of like it being just you and me."

"Me too."

"We won't tell Mom. Plus, she needs her beauty sleep to beat me in tennis later."

Jules loved watching us play. She'd pull a chair by the net and call out the score.

Darla didn't know it wouldn't be for much longer, or that Jules really needed her beauty sleep for the baby growing inside her.

Darla giggled as I hoisted her back into the kayak. "I'm going to get a pineapple-banana smoothie. How 'bout you, Dad?"

I climbed in, then picked up the paddle and turned us back toward shore. "Sounds good to me. Can we share?"

"Nope."

"Hey, Darla?"

"Yeah, Daddy?"

"Remember the first time I bought you a strawberry smoothie at Rocky Brook?"

She nodded. "After my first lesson with you."

"I loved you then as much as I love you now. I fell for you in an instant."

"Me too. I wished that day to have you as my daddy."

Those words were even more spectacular than the killer whale cresting on the horizon.

Later that night, with Darla out cold and tucked into her bed, the ocean air doing its magic, I brought Jules a sparkling water with lemon. We had a suite with two rooms despite Jules arguing over it. I wanted her to get rest, and I wanted to *service* her. This pregnancy had made her horny as fuck.

Considering I missed the whole shebang with Darla, my plan was to attend to every detail of this one. Especially the horny part.

From the moment Jules told me, the day before we left for Hawaii, I'd been on cloud nine. It was better than making a million, better than anything.

"Thanks," she said from the sofa in the common area of our suite.

"Want anything else?"

She shook her head and curled into the corner, patting the cushion next to her.

That's right, I obliged.

"Having a good time?" I asked, taking her foot in my hand.

"Mmm," melted from her mouth. "Not as good as you. Snorkeling, kayaking, water slides, buying Darla big smoothies in those fake pineapple cups. I'd say you're having the most fun."

"You won at tennis today," I said, trying to console her.

She giggled. "Because you let me."

"No way."

"Drew, you did. You barely made a forehand."

"I just like watching you run around with these new tits." This earned me a pinch on the arm. "Breasts, new and improved breasts," I said, correcting myself.

"Seriously, you have a one-track mind." Her eyes sparkled almost as much as the water in the glass.

"It's like a switch in me. As soon as Darla is quiet, I crave you."

Jules didn't respond, only set her drink down, leaned forward, and pressed her lips to mine. "Me too."

"Before I have my way with you, how about running into Hilary and Stacia today? Wasn't that a blast from the past? Guess we're in the hot place

218

to be at Christmas. You sure you can handle that? All the attention?" I tickled her side. "How they practically jumped out of their lily-white skin when they caught us kissing by the pool?"

"Uh, it was a bit embarrassing. Especially when they saw Darla and said, 'You're not Lamar's baby.'"

My lips glided over hers. "I can't believe they thought that all these years. She's mine, all mine. And you."

"And thank God you're mine. Not sure I could put up with those lawyer sticks-in-the-muds they ended up with. Didn't they feel so Stepford wife-y to you?"

I chuckled into her ear. "No one could accuse you of being Stepford wife-y for sure."

"I know we were never that close, but still. They seemed too plastic and perfect."

"Not my type. I like all fire and brimstone."

She slapped my bicep. "Cut it out. Seriously, they were aghast and then they started with all the *He did always favor you* and *We should have known.* It was so embarrassing."

"I could have really embarrassed you and them . . ."

"Pretty sure you did that when you stuck your naughty tongue in my mouth poolside."

I pushed her hair away from her face and held her still, her cheeks in my hands. "Who cares? I love you so much, Jules King."

Her nose rubbed against mine. "Right back at you, Coach King."

"Who's naughty now?"

I didn't allow her to answer. I couldn't wait to have my way with her.

EXTENDED EPILOGUE

Jules

"Hey, Mom, I'm home," echoed through the house.

"Carla's here," James yelled from the downstairs TV room.

"She's going to kill you if you keep up that stupid name game," I hollered back to him.

"Hey, loser, I see you're doing what your loser-ish self always does. Video games." Darla chuckled as she made her way into the TV room.

I watched silently from the top of the stairs.

"I'll have you know, Marla, I met a gamer girl who digs me and my video games. We're playing right now."

"What do you know about girls? You're thirteen."

I made my way down and sat on the bottom step, leaning against the wall as I listened to my two kids bicker. It was heaven to me. Having them both home was like winning a singles match.

Or having sex in peace, which didn't happen often, but fast, messy sex was good too.

I wasn't sure it was always so peaceful for them. Poor Darla, having a brother eight years younger. He couldn't say Darla when he was a toddler.

220

It started out as "Arla," but when he got older, he'd add any combination of consonants to it but *D*.

"I have an older sister named Starla, so I know a lot about girls," he shot back.

"How you doing, tough guy?" Darla bent over and ruffled the top of his dark blond bed head.

Summer vacation had just started for James, and I'd been counting the minutes for Darla to come home for a few weeks. She'd just finished her junior year and her third season playing tennis at the University of Miami. She could have gone on the national circuit, but becoming a marine veterinarian took precedence. She got the big D-1 scholarship, and after that was set to devote herself to the health of dolphins and turtles and Lord knew what else. Not the type of doctor I'd told her she could be when she was little, but even more impressive in our minds. I credit most of her achievements to Drew constantly telling her she could do anything.

"Pretty good. Made honor roll."

"Good. Should do it every semester, little bro. What about swimming?"

I chuckled at that. Darla had been his second mother since he was born, doting on him, seeing to his every need, pushing him to be the best.

"Swimming for the team at Rocky Brook this summer. Getting ready for eighth grade."

"You've got to be the best to swim in high school. This is Florida, so don't let up."

"Yeah, yeah. Can I unpause my game now?"

"Yep. Where's Mom?"

"Right here." I sneaked out from the corner where I'd been eavesdropping.

We still lived in the coastal house. I could never leave it. We'd remodeled and added two additions, but it was home. I was going to die here, no matter what Drew said.

"Hey, Mom!" Darla squeezed me tight.

"Hey, baby girl." I shoved the hair out of her face. She wore her strawberry-blond locks down, wispy strips flying all around her face.

"Leave it, Mom. It doesn't bother me. Do you like it flat ironed?" She tugged on my loose bun, setting my waves free. "I see you don't mind throwing caution to the wind either," she said as she tousled my hair.

"Ha. Where's your stuff?"

"It's in the car. I didn't bring it in yet because . . . well, there's one thing I didn't mention."

I froze. "What, Darla?"

My mind went through five billion scenarios in thirty seconds. Yes, Darla was smart and a talented tennis player, but she wasn't without fault. There'd been a sea turtle in our saltwater pool for a week, a litter of puppies living in our garage, and a major blowout party her senior year when Drew and I had gone home for my mother's funeral.

"I brought someone home with me."

"Darla, that's fine. You know you're always welcome to have company, even if it's a boy. I'm not naive."

"But I am," James called out, and I shushed him.

Darla fidgeted, not meeting my eyes. "Well, it's a boy, but there are some extenuating circumstances. Can we go into the kitchen?"

"Don't mind me," James piped in again.

"Mom?"

"Come on."

Part of me wished Drew were home. He'd been much better over the years at dealing with Darla's antics. He was so patient, always making up for lost time.

"What is it?" I asked as soon as we were seated at the kitchen island, pots and pans dangling from the rack above.

"It sort of has to stay on the DL, and I know you'll understand."

"Just spit it out, Darla."

"I'm dating this guy—"

"That's pretty normal for your age, I think."

"Mom, stop interrupting. Actually, I'm crazy for this guy, and he's nuts for me."

"Great. I can't wait to meet him. What the heck is he doing out there?"

"Well, I don't think you should be alarmed by this. Especially you. He's my coach."

My tongue went dry and my throat hoarse.

222

"Mom, you know you can't start."

I nodded, casting about furiously for something to say. "Um, are you sure? You're risking a lot. He's risking a lot."

"He was thinking if he had yours and Dad's approval, he would look for a job at a private club. We could live together, and he could coach me on the side."

"Oh God, Dar. This is too much." I pulled her in for a hug. "Let's meet the guy to begin with. And for the record, I'm not starting, but thank God your dad's at work, because he's gonna start."

"So, can Aaron come inside?"

I should have known Aaron Brown was going to be a problem the moment I saw his young ass strut onto the court. His arrival made a splash at U of Miami during Darla's sophomore year, him being all tall, lean, tanned, and dark-headed. Every girl on the team was batting their eyelashes at him, charmed by his Southern twang. Of course, only my daughter turned out to be his darling.

"Are you sure you're ready for this, baby girl?"

"I'm so sure, but is there any chance Dad has a business trip or something coming up?"

"No chance. In fact, in about an hour or two, poor Aaron will hear 'No one is good enough for my superstar.'"

ACKNOWLEDGMENTS

Thank you to my family. After eight books, you still put up with my frantic pre- and post-release frenzies, love me, adore me, and feed me. I love you more than I can ever put into words, and that says it all.

This includes my Electric Readers. *You're family.* I can't imagine a day without waking up and going to sleep with you.

To Pam Berehulke, my editor, friend, and trusted confidante. I'm sure this story gave you many gray hairs. Originally, I said, "It's only a novella," and then I changed my mind. Thanks, Pammy, for rolling with it. Love you hard!

As always, Sarah Hansen of Okay Creations took whatever was in my head and put it on a cover. I'm forever indebted.

To Nicole, my trusted PA. Don't ever let anyone tell you that you can't be a better me. :) Ha! You are who makes my whole world tick.

To Queen V, my very first friend in the book world. I am so happy to see your book services business grow, and proud that you proofread this book baby.

To my early readers, Jennifer D and Terilyn S, you're the secret sauce. Thank you for all you do every day on the battlefield.

A special thanks to Robin B and Jennifer W for lending advice, constructive criticism, and making me cry once or twice with every book.

To Eric Battershell and Burton Hughes, thank you for the gorgeous photograph. Mostly thanks to Burton's lovely wife, Kaitlin, who supports our industry without bounds.

Lisa Schilling Hintz, there are no words. None. It took me a while, but I found a partner in crime in releasing books. Thank you to you and all of the TRSOR peeps.

It's impossible to thank every author friend and not leave someone out.

There are many of you who are new, and even more who are old. I love you all. Without you, it would be a lonely life.

And to the heartbeat of the indie book world—the bloggers. *You, you, and you* make it all happen. Thank you, thank you, thank you.

ABOUT THE AUTHOR

Rachel Blaufeld is a bestselling author of Romantic Suspense, New Adult, Coming-of-Age Romance, and Sports Romance. A recent poll of her readers described her as *insightful, generous, articulate,* and *spunky*. Originally a social worker, Rachel creates broken yet redeeming characters. She's been known to turn up the angst like cranking up the heat in the dead of winter.

A devout coffee drinker and doughnut eater, Rachel spends way too many hours in local coffee shops, downing the aforementioned goodies while she plots her ideas. Her tales may all come with a side of angst and naughtiness, but end as lusciously as her treats.

As a side note, Blaufeld, also a long-time blogger and an advocate of woman-run anything, is fearless about sharing her opinion. She captured the ears of stay-at-home and working moms on her blog, *BacknGrooveMom*, chronicling her adventures in parenting tweens and running a business, often at the same time. To her, work/life/family balance is an urban legend, but she does her best.

Rachel has also blogged for *The Huffington Post* and *Modern Mom*. Most recently, her insights can be found in *USA TODAY,* where she shares conversations at "In Bed with a Romance Author" and reading recommendations over at "Happy Ever After."

Rachel lives around the corner from her childhood home in Pennsylvania with her family and two beagles. Her obsessions include running, coffee, basketball, icing-filled doughnuts, antiheroes, and mighty fine epilogues.

When she isn't writing, she can be found courtside, tweeting about hoops as her son plays, or walking around the house wearing earplugs while her other son, the drummer, bangs away.

To connect with Rachel, she's most active in her private reading group, *The Electric Readers*, where she shares insider information and intimate conversation with her readers:

www.facebook.com/groups/TunnelVIPS

As well as:

www.rachelblaufeld.com
twitter.com/rachelblaufeld
www.facebook.com/rachelblaufeldtheauthor
www.rachelblaufeld.com/signup

If you liked this book, feel free to leave a review where you bought it or on Goodreads. Send me an e-mail when you do, and I will thank you personally!